FRIEND INDEED?

"How did you like your first morning?" Jana asked Lizzie as they sat down with their lunch trays.

Lizzie shrugged and stabbed at her meatball. "It was all right," she said, "if you like boredom."

"Yeah, it can be boring, all right," Jana said. "But sometimes it's really fun. There are a lot of activities you can get involved in. I'm the seventh-grade co-editor of our school yearbook. Some of my friends are cheerleaders and in the school plays."

"Uh-huh," Lizzie said, looking very bored.

"Maybe you'd like to get involved in some of those activities," Jana added hopefully.

"Yeah, right," Lizzie said sarcastically.

"It was just a suggestion," Jana said in a small voice. "Maybe you'll like your afternoon classes better, Lizzie."

Lizzie sat back in her chair and gazed at Jana for a moment. "Would you do me a favor, Jana?"

"Sure," Jana said, eager to help.

"Would you call me Liz instead of Lizzie?"

"Oh, sure, okay," Jana said.

Lizzie nodded and folded her arms across her chest. "Just my good friends call me Lizzie."

THE FABULOUS FIVE

Jana to the Rescue

BETSY HAYNES

A BANTAM SKYLARK BOOK
NEW YORK · TORONTO · LONDON · SYDNEY · AUCKLAND

RL 5, 009–012

JANA TO THE RESCUE
A Bantam Skylark Book / November 1990

ISBN 0-553-15840-6

Published simultaneously in the United States and Canada

PRINTED IN THE UNITED STATES OF AMERICA

OPM   0 9 8 7 6 5 4 3 2 1

Jana
to the
Rescue

CHAPTER

1

Jana Morgan hurried down the hall, clutching the note in her hand. It had been delivered to her just moments ago from the principal's office, and she couldn't imagine what it meant.

The note was printed on a slip of yellow paper, and it looked like a multiple-choice test.

_x_ *Please see the principal, Mr. Bell.*
____ *Please see the counselor, Mrs. Brenner.*
____ *Please see the office secretary, Miss Simone.*
____ *Please see the nurse, Miss Byars.*

_x_ *Immediately.*
____ *After your next class.*
____ *During lunch.*
____ *After school.*

1

Jana wondered why Mr. Bell wanted to see her. Usually he used the yellow slip to summon troublemakers, but she certainly was not a troublemaker. In fact, she was a good student, and her teachers seemed to like her a lot.

Miss Simone, the school secretary, was sitting at her desk, talking on the phone, when Jana walked into the office.

"Hi, Jana. You got a yellow slip, too?"

Jana glanced to the left and saw Whitney Larkin and four other students sitting in a row of chairs along the wall. Whitney was also a seventh-grader. Tim Riggs and Shelly Bramlett were eighth-graders, and Kyle Zimmerman and Pam Wolthoff were in ninth. All of them were good students and definitely not troublemakers, which made her feel a little better.

"I sure did," answered Jana. She motioned toward the others. "Did everybody get the same slip?"

Whitney nodded. "No one can figure it out."

"I wondered if I was in trouble for a minute," Jana said.

"Oh, so did I," Whitney said. "Or if they'd changed the rules about skipping grades and that I would have to go back to the sixth." She rolled her eyes as if to say that would be the pits.

Jana smiled. Whitney was not only one of the smartest seventh-graders in Wacko, she was probably a genius. That was why she had gotten to move from fifth grade directly into seventh this year. She was smaller than most seventh-graders, and for a while some kids had resented her and treated her like a baby.

Just then the door to the principal's office opened, and Mr. Bell stepped out with the counselor, Mrs. Brenner. They were both smiling.

"Come with us, everybody," Mr. Bell said cheerfully. "There's no one in the cafeteria now. We can talk there."

The students shuffled down the hall behind Mr. Bell and Mrs. Brenner, shrugging and looking quizzically at one another. Jana was as puzzled as everyone else, but at least she wasn't worried anymore.

When they reached the cafeteria, Mr. Bell pointed to one of the long picnic-style tables. "Have a seat, folks," he said. When they were settled, he went on. "You're probably curious about why I called all of you in today."

"Yeah, Mr. Bell," piped up Tim Riggs. He grinned. "We thought we were in *deeeeep* trouble."

Mr. Bell smiled. "Oh, just the opposite. In fact, you were chosen to come in here today because you are good students, you get along well with other kids, and your teachers think you are sensitive to the needs of others."

"Boy," said Tim, talking to the kids around the table, "I guess we fooled *them*, huh?"

Everyone laughed at Tim, then turned back to the principal.

"I think you are all familiar with our buddy system for new students," Mr. Bell said. "Whenever a student comes in during the school year, we pair that person up with another student who can, in general, be a friend while the new girl or boy is getting acclimated."

"Right," said Kyle Zimmerman. "I was paired with two different kids last year. It was fun, and both of them turned out to be good friends."

Mr. Bell nodded. "Well, we're going to start a new program that is nearly identical to that," he said, "but the students will be from Phoenix House."

"The shelter for the homeless?" Pam asked, and a low murmur went through the room.

"Yes," said Mr. Bell. "You probably have heard about the number of homeless people we have in this town."

The kids nodded. Jana remembered about a month ago when the local TV station aired a report on the plight of the homeless in their area. The reporter had been Marge Whitworth, her friend Jon Smith's mother, and the program had startled Jana. She had been shocked that there were so many people right around her own home who didn't have a place to live or enough food. Marge Whitworth had pointed out that the homeless were all colors, sizes, and ages. But the most surprising thing she said was that half of the people who lived in homeless shelters were children. Jana had thought for a long time about that. She had always supposed that most of the people who wound up in shelters were winos or drug addicts or people with mental problems, not kids.

Mr. Bell nodded toward the counselor. "Mrs. Brenner will tell you about the experimental program we're going to start here at Wakeman to mainstream the junior high age kids of these families. Some of the younger children will go into similar programs at two of the local elementary schools."

"Hey, that's a great idea," said Tim Riggs. Jana agreed with him.

Mrs. Brenner stood at the end of the table and looked at each of the students. "If any of you have ever moved to a new school, you know how difficult it is to fit in when you don't know anyone."

"That's sure true," Kyle said. "I moved here in fifth grade, and I was totally miserable for the first six months."

Mrs. Brenner nodded sympathetically. "Well, just imagine how you would feel if you were also homeless."

Again, the image of drunk old men and druggies flashed in Jana's mind. But what would it be like if *she* were homeless? It could have happened. The thought shocked her. But it was true. Her father had deserted her mother and her when she was only three. He had almost never sent support checks, and her mother had had to support them as best she could by herself until a few months ago when she remarried. What if she hadn't been able to get a job? What if . . .

Mr. Bell's voice interrupted her thoughts. "We'd like to pair up each homeless student with one of you people if you like the idea, and you'll all be part of this new buddy system. The new students will be scheduled into most—but not all—of your classes. You will have the opportunity to show them around, help them with class work if they need it, eat lunch with them, and just generally be a friend and assist them in any way you can."

The room was silent for a moment.

Jana felt emotion welling up inside. If things had worked out differently, I could have been one of them, she thought. "I think it's a *terrific* idea," she said more loudly than she had meant to. In a softer voice she added, "It'll be fun, and we'll make some new friends."

Suddenly all around the table the kids started nodding and buzzing with conversation about the project.

"Now, this won't be easy," Mrs. Brenner warned. "Most of these kids will be behind in their subjects. In fact, a lot of them will have missed weeks or even months of school because of their situation. When you don't have a home, it's pretty tough to go to school or to get schoolwork done."

"Well, what do you think?" asked Mr. Bell. "Do the rest of you like the idea?"

"I like it," piped up Tim.

"Me, too," said Whitney.

"Yeah, it's gonna be cool," said Kyle.

"Is there anyone here who would prefer not to participate?" asked Mrs. Brenner.

The chatter at the table stopped abruptly, and the boys and girls looked around questioningly at one another, but no one spoke.

"Okay, great," Mr. Bell said, smiling.

"Will guys be paired with guys and girls with girls?" asked Kyle.

Mr. Bell chuckled. "I'm afraid so, Kyle."

"Rats," said Kyle, snapping his fingers in make-believe disappointment. The others laughed.

"When do the new kids get here?" asked Whitney.

"Right away," Mr. Bell replied. "In fact, some of them will be here tomorrow. The rest will arrive by the end of the week."

"Keep in mind, though, that homeless people often don't stay in one place very long," interjected Mrs. Brenner. "There may be students who start school at Wakeman and then leave in a few months or weeks—or in some cases, even days. But others will come in to take their places."

"How will we know when our student has arrived?" asked Jana.

"The office will send you a note to come down and meet your partner," Mr. Bell said. "Any more questions?"

Heads shook around the table.

"Okay," he said. "If you need help, don't hesitate to come in and see me or Mrs. Brenner."

Jana left the cafeteria with the rest of the students. She felt good about the buddy system and was flattered that her teachers thought enough of her to suggest her for the program.

But one thing nagged at her a little. How would the rest of The Fabulous Five feel about her spending most of her time with the new student? They were super friends and would surely understand, but Mr. Bell had said that most of her classes would include the new girl. She would have to walk to classes with her, eat lunch with her, do all kinds of things with her. That wouldn't leave much time for anyone else. Would her friends really understand?

CHAPTER

2

"But that's crazy!" Katie Shannon said. "We don't mind. In fact, this sounds like a great program. Here's a chance for us kids to really *do* something to help the homeless."

"That's right," said Beth Barry, nodding. She turned to Jana. "Of course, we don't mind."

"Right," Christie Winchell echoed.

"You're sure?" Jana said. "You know, the new girl will need an awful lot of my time."

"Of course we don't want to be without you," Christie said, "so why not just invite her to join all of us at lunch? And if we're going the same direction to classes, we'll all walk together."

Jana sighed with relief and sagged against the chain-link fence that surrounded the school property. She should have known her friends wouldn't mind. The Fabulous Five stuck together, no matter what.

"You don't know how good this makes me feel," she said.

"Oh, Jana, you shouldn't have worried about us," said Beth. "But what about Randy? Do you think he'll be jealous?"

"He'd better not be," interrupted Katie. "He has no more claim to your time than anyone else."

"I know," Jana admitted. "And he's really a sensitive and caring person, so I hope he likes the idea. It would make it a lot easier for me." She stopped and glanced around. "Say, has anyone seen Melanie?"

"Gosh, no," said Beth. "I wonder where she is?"

This spot by the fence was the usual meeting place for The Fabulous Five before school.

"Maybe she's sick," offered Katie.

Beth squinted off into the distance. "Isn't that her coming now?"

Jana followed Beth's gaze and saw Melanie Edwards running—her arms and legs pumping hard—in their direction along the sidewalk.

"She sure is in a hurry," Beth said. "I wonder what's up?"

It took Melanie another minute to reach them. Gasping for breath, she staggered up to her four friends and collapsed against the fence, causing the chain-link to thwang against the framing pole.

"Melanie, are you okay?" Jana asked.

Melanie nodded while she tried to catch her breath.

"Hey, you weren't late or anything," Beth assured her. "What's the rush?"

"Test," Melanie said between breaths. "I have this test."

"You have a test today?" asked Jana. "You were studying and left for school late?" It was beginning to be like a game trying to find out what Melanie's problem was.

Melanie shook her head. "I had to make copies before I left," she said.

"You made *copies* of a school test?" Katie asked, her voice rising in alarm. "I thought you knew better—"

"No," Melanie interrupted, her breathing beginning to return to normal. "It's not a school test. I swear. I got it in the mail yesterday from my cousin in California."

"What kind of test?" asked Jana.

"It's totally awesome," Melanie said, her eyes wide. "Here, let me show you."

Melanie dug through her book bag for a full minute.

"Oh, rats, where are they?" she mumbled. "I worked all through breakfast . . . Oh, here they are!" She pulled out a handful of papers. "It's about getting your *true love*!" she announced proudly.

Katie groaned. "Are you kidding?"

"No, I'm completely serious about this," Melanie said, shuffling through the papers. Then she stopped and looked up at Katie. "This is not a joking matter, Katie. My cousin tried the test, and it *worked*!"

Katie rolled her eyes.

"Let me see it, Mel," said Jana.

Melanie handed the papers to Jana, who glanced quickly over the six sheets.

"These are all the same," said Jana. "I don't get it."

"I know," Melanie said. "You're supposed to send out these tests to six girls within six days—"

"You mean like a chain letter?" asked Beth.

Melanie shrugged. "Sort of. What you do is send out these tests to six girls in six days. Then on the fourth day after that, you drink a glass of water, then say your favorite guy's name. Within another four days, he'll ask you out or tell you he likes you. If you get the letter and *don't* do what it says, your love life during the next *four years* will be a total disaster!"

Katie, Christie, and Beth burst out laughing. Jana wanted to, but she was able to control herself.

"That's the silliest thing I ever heard," said Katie.

Beth stopped giggling long enough to ask, "Does it work if you drink Pepsi instead of water?"

Melanie frowned and stomped her foot. "I'm perfectly serious! I know it sounds a little crazy, but can you imagine if it works? Wouldn't that be super?"

"So, what's in the test?" asked Christie.

"It's all about the things you should think about before you drink the water and say the name," Melanie said. "Like"—she began reading—"'What qualities do you want your boyfriend to have?' Now that makes sense! I'll bet a psychologist or somebody who really knows about relationships wrote this test."

Katie laughed again, but Christie gave her a nudge with her elbow, so she covered her mouth with her hand and tried to keep a straight face.

"And, 'How important are his looks?'" Melanie read. She stopped and stared off into the distance, thinking. "Got a pen or pencil?"

Jana handed her a ballpoint pen.

"Ve-ry im-por-tant," Melanie said as she wrote.

"Oh, brother," said Katie.

"These are all important," Melanie said defensively. "Here, you four take a test."

"No way," said Katie, shaking her head.

"Us, either," the others said in unison.

Melanie shrugged. "Suit yourself," she said. Then she grinned slyly. "But you may never find your true love."

Katie grinned back. "I'll take my chances," she said.

"Okay, but I've got to give these tests to six girls before the end of the six days," Melanie said.

"I'm sure you'll find some kids who'll think it's fun," Jana assured her, "even if they don't quite believe it."

"Yeah," Melanie said. "I should quit worrying. I'll find some girls who'll take it seriously." She directed the last comment to Katie, who just smiled.

"So when does your new student show up?" Beth asked, turning back to Jana.

"Anytime," Jana said. "Maybe even today."

"New student?" asked Melanie, wrinkling her nose. "What's that all about?"

"Wacko is hosting some homeless kids," Jana explained. "I'm getting paired up with one of them."

"Wow. Do you think it might be a *boy*?" Melanie asked, her eyes getting wide.

Jana shook her head. "Girls are paired with girls."

"Have you ever noticed," said Beth, "that when Melanie talks about boys, the pupils of her eyes dilate?"

Melanie burst into fits of giggles. "Really?"

"Really," Beth answered, grinning.

Just then the first bell rang, and students began heading toward the building.

"Come on," Jana said. "If my student is here, I want to be available whenever the office sends for me."

"Oh, and I've got to find some girls to take the test," Melanie said. "It would be *horrible* if I had to go through four years of a disastrous love life."

Jana shook her head as they hurried into the school building and scattered to their classes.

*   *   *

For the next two days, Jana could hardly think of anything else but the new girl she would be paired with. She kept waiting to be called to the office to meet her, but the call hadn't come.

Several of the new students had arrived already. She had seen Whitney Larkin escorting a new girl between classes, but she hadn't had a chance to speak to Whitney about how it was going.

Sitting in her first period history class on Thursday, Jana made a mental note to call Whitney that night. Then she started daydreaming about the girl who would be assigned to her. Jana wondered what her name would be, whether she would be nice, and whether they would have things in common. But most of all, Jana was excited about the idea of helping this new girl. She knew that it wouldn't be easy at times, but she expected good things to happen. After all, she reasoned, she really wanted to help.

Jana sat at her desk and doodled on her notebook. Then she started making a list of things she could do for the girl on her first day. She'd already decided that she wouldn't overwhelm the girl by introducing her to The Fabulous Five right away. Jana knew that she and the new girl would want to have a little time alone first to get to know each other.

Jana began her list.

1. *Show her to locker.*
2. *Introduce her to teachers.*
3. *Eat lunch alone with her.*

Jana paused and tapped her pencil against her cheek. That all seemed so obvious. What else could she do? She couldn't think of anything.

The classroom door opening caught her eye, and a student messenger from the office strode across the front of the room and handed Mr. Naset a note.

Jana's stomach fluttered and she sat up straight. Was the office sending for her?

"Jana," said Mr. Naset, looking up from the note. "Your presence is requested in the office."

Jana gasped, leaped to her feet, and headed for the door. Oh, she thought, maybe I should bring my books and stuff in case I don't have time to come back—

She whirled around and headed back for her desk, then stopped. She'll be in most of my classes anyway, she thought. I'll be coming back to history.

She turned for the door and stopped again. But if I'm gone for the rest of the period, I'll need my books to go on to second period, she reasoned.

She sighed and whirled around for the third time, causing the kids around her to laugh. Rushing back to her desk, she grabbed her book bag and pencils.

"You look like a duck in a shooting gallery! Calm down," Beth whispered loudly behind her hand. "You'll be fine."

Jana's cheeks turned red, but she managed to flash a weak smile at Beth and then ran out the door.

CHAPTER

3

*W*hat should I say to her? Jana wondered. She wished she had written a list of things she could talk about in her first meeting with the new girl.

Oh, well, I guess I'll play it by ear, she decided. Just let it happen.

She rushed into the girls' bathroom and ran a brush through her hair. She wanted to make a good first impression.

Outside the office door, Jana stopped and took a deep, calming breath. Then another. Okay, she thought, I'm as ready as I'll ever be. She opened the door.

Miss Simone looked up from her desk. "Ah, Jana," she said, smiling, "Mr. Bell and Mrs. Brenner are waiting for you in Mr. Bell's office."

"Thanks," said Jana. She steadied herself and walked in.

"Hi, Jana," Mr. Bell said cordially. "Come in and sit down." He gestured to an empty seat next to his desk. Jana sat down.

Sitting around the principal's office were three adults: Mr. Bell, Mrs. Brenner, the counselor, and a pale, thin woman with dark hair.

Sitting next to the woman was a girl about Jana's age. She was rather pretty, Jana thought, with large, dark eyes and shoulder-length brown hair, although her hair looked as if it needed shampooing. She wore a faded pair of jeans and a worn red jacket that was unzipped, revealing a plaid shirt underneath. On her feet were ancient, worn-out sneakers. She was flexing her feet nervously, and Jana noticed that one of the shoes was coming apart at the front toe seam. The one detail that didn't go with the rest of her was the pair of earrings she was wearing. They looked like real gold and were among the prettiest Jana had seen. The girl's gaze swept quickly over Jana, then she looked at the floor.

"Jana," Mr. Bell said, "this is Lizzie Flagg and her mother. Lizzie's starting school here at Wakeman today."

"Hi," Jana said, and smiled.

Lizzie looked up at Jana and softly said, "Hi." She didn't return the smile.

"Well," said Mr. Bell. "Mrs. Brenner and I have worked out Lizzie's schedule to fit with yours, Jana.

The only class she'll have that will be different from yours is biology, which you don't have. That'll give her a chance to meet some new people on her own."

"Okay," said Jana cheerfully.

She looked at Lizzie, who seemed incredibly bored as she stared out the window, yawning. Mr. Bell looked around the room, and his gaze stopped at Lizzie's mother.

"Do you have any questions for us, Mrs. Flagg?" he asked.

Mrs. Flagg shook her head but didn't speak. Jana studied her closely. Was she bored, too? No, it was something else, Jana decided. She looked tired, incredibly frazzled, as if it took all her effort to sit in the chair.

"How about you, Lizzie?" Mr. Bell asked.

Lizzie also shook her head.

"Well then, I think I'll excuse you two young ladies. Jana, you should show Lizzie to her locker first, then go to your class."

"Here's Lizzie's locker number," said Mrs. Brenner. She handed Jana a slip of paper.

Mr. Bell stood up. He reached out to shake Lizzie's hand, but she only stared at him, keeping her hand by her side.

"Welcome to Wakeman, Lizzie," he said, slowly lowering his own hand. "I'm sure you'll like it here. Your locker combination is printed on your schedule card that Mrs. Brenner gave you."

Lizzie nodded slightly.

"I didn't hear the bell," Jana said as she stood up. "Are we still in first period?"

"Period one will be ending in a few minutes," the principal said. "If you hurry, you'll have time to stop by Lizzie's locker on your way to second period class."

The two girls moved out the door and into the outer office. Jana opened the door for Lizzie to go into the hall, but the girl didn't move.

I don't like the way this is starting out, Jana thought, biting her lower lip. But she didn't say anything. Instead she hurried into the hall and was relieved to see Lizzie trailing along behind her.

"I think you'll like Wakeman Junior High," Jana said, slowing slightly to let Lizzie catch up. "Actually, most of the kids call it Wacko." She laughed a little, and Lizzie glanced at her quickly but didn't respond.

"The teachers here are really nice," Jana continued, trying desperately to make conversation as they walked down the hall. "You'll especially like Miss Dickinson, our English teacher."

Jana thought she saw Lizzie nod.

The bell rang then, ending the first period, and within seconds, the hall was crowded with seventh-, eighth-, and ninth-graders hurrying to their next classes.

"I remember I was really nervous on the first day of junior high," Jana said quickly. She knew she was talking too fast, but she couldn't help it. Lizzie's silence was getting to her. "But once you get to know some of the other kids and the teachers, and you get involved in school activities, you'll think it's great!"

Lizzie glanced sideways at Jana, then muttered, "Did anyone ever tell you, you talk too much?"

Jana was stunned. "I wanted to tell you about Wakeman," she said in a small voice. "There are some things you'll have to know."

Lizzie stared straight ahead and didn't respond.

Jana didn't speak for a full minute—at least it seemed like at least a minute—but then realized that she *had* to tell her about some of the day-to-day details about Wakeman.

"Your locker is right around here somewhere," Jana said. She scanned the long rows of lockers that ran down either side of the hall. "Number twenty-three nineteen. Oh, here it is."

Jana walked up to the tall, narrow locker painted pale blue and turned to Lizzie. A passing student jostled Lizzie, who scowled and pressed her shoulder up next to the lockers to avoid contact with any more kids.

"Do you have your schedule card?" Jana asked.

Lizzie nodded but didn't move.

"Your combination is printed on the top right corner," Jana said.

Lizzie frowned but still didn't move.

Jana couldn't understand why Lizzie didn't open her locker. "Do you want to hang up your jacket?"

she asked, trying hard not to let the exasperation she was feeling be heard in her voice.

"I want to *wear* my jacket, okay?" Lizzie's voice was thick with hostility.

Jana winced. "Sure, okay," she said. "I just thought you might like to open your locker and make sure the combination's right. Once in a while, the office makes a mistake or the locker sticks. If it's not okay, we can get it fixed right away."

"No," Lizzie said, her voice a little softer.

Jana nodded and forced herself to smile.

"Okay," she said. "Maybe we'd better get to your biology class so that I can introduce you to Mr. Dracovitch. We have just five minutes between classes, so you'll always have to hurry if you're going to stop at your locker or the bathroom."

The two girls walked down the hall in silence. One minute Jana wanted to scream in frustration. The next, she wanted to stomp off and let Lizzie find her way around by herself. But she knew she couldn't do either. This is what this project is all about, she reminded herself. Helping kids like Lizzie feel at home in a strange school.

"Hi, Jana!" Alexis Duvall called out as she passed them.

"Hi, Alexis," Jana answered.

"Wait till you take that math test," Alexis shouted over the noise. "It's a killer!"

Lizzie hadn't even looked up to see the girl who spoke. She kept her eyes directly on the floor.

"Oh, here's your biology class," Jana said. "Mr. Dracovitch is a little weird, but everybody loves his class."

Jana led the way into the classroom, then turned to speak to Lizzie.

"Come up front, and I'll introduce you," she said.

The classroom was already crowded with kids. Jana walked briskly between two rows of seats up to the front of the classroom. The teacher was writing on the board, his back to her.

"Excuse me, Mr. Dracovitch," Jana said.

The tall, slender man turned around. The paleness of his skin and the black, shiny toupee that always sat too far forward on his head made all the kids think of Dracula. In fact, everyone even called him Dracula behind his back.

Jana and the rest of The Fabulous Five had thought that he didn't know what the kids called him. But not long ago they discovered that he *wanted* the kids to think of him as Dracula in order to get them interested in coming to his class and studying science.

"Yes, Jana," he said.

"I'd like you to meet your new student, Lizzie Flagg," Jana began. She turned around to gesture to Lizzie, but Lizzie wasn't there.

"Lizzie?"

"A phantom student, Jana?" Mr. Dracovitch said, smiling devilishly. "Sounds like my kind of person."

Jana couldn't help grinning. "She was here just a minute ago." "Excuse me, I'll be right back."

Jana rushed down between the rows of desks to the back of the room. Students were milling around, chatting and getting ready for class to begin.

"Lizzie!" Jana found Lizzie still standing in the doorway, gazing into the hall. "Come up and meet Mr. Dracovitch."

Lizzie frowned but followed Jana up to the front of the classroom.

"This is Lizzie Flagg," Jana said in a controlled voice. "She's new today and has some classes with me, so I'm showing her around."

"Hello, Lizzie," Mr. Dracovitch said. "Glad to have you join us. I think there's an empty seat in the back. You can sit there."

Lizzie shrugged. "Okay."

She trudged to the desk located in the back of the classroom, close to a window, and sat down. She stuffed her hands into the pockets of her jacket. Jana hurried to her own class, relieved to get there and face an entire class period without having to try to make conversation with Lizzie.

The morning classes seemed to drag for Jana. She had known that Lizzie might not be superfriendly, but this was ridiculous. She was surprised and hurt at how hostile and angry Lizzie actually was. Jana kept wondering what more she could do to make this new school experience go smoothly for Lizzie.

At lunchtime, Jana led Lizzie to the cafeteria and

showed her where to get in the hot-lunch line. Jana paid for her own lunch, and then Lizzie leaned far over to the side to block Jana's view. Jana could still see, though, when Lizzie took out a card and slipped it in front of the woman selling lunch tickets. The woman glanced at the card and nodded, and then turned to the boy behind Lizzie to get his lunch money.

She didn't want me to see that she's on the free lunch program, Jana thought. That made Jana sad. There were quite a few low-income kids getting reduced or free lunches, and it wasn't a big deal. She had always thought it was a great program, that kids could always get a hot lunch, no matter how much their parents earned.

"Let's sit over by the window," Jana said when they had their lunch trays.

She smiled and waved at The Fabulous Five at their usual table. She'd told each of them that on the new girl's first day she would sit alone with her at lunch. Her friends had agreed that it would be a good idea for Jana to spend some private time with her at first.

"How did you like your first morning?" Jana asked Lizzie after they'd sat down.

Lizzie shrugged and took a stab at the meatball on her spaghetti. "It was all right," she said, "if you like boredom."

"Yeah, it *can* be boring, all right," Jana said. "But sometimes it's really fun. Mr. Dracovitch, for instance, can be really interesting. Once he had his classes dissect a cow's eyeball!"

Lizzie dropped her fork with the meatball back into her plate.

"Oops, sorry," Jana said, and giggled nervously. "I shouldn't have mentioned that at lunch."

Lizzie made a face. "That's disgusting," she mumbled.

"But what I meant was that Wakeman doesn't have to be boring," Jana insisted. "There are a lot of activities you can get involved in, too. I'm the seventh-grade coeditor of *The Wigwam*, our school yearbook. Some of my friends are cheerleaders and in the school plays and on the Teen Court."

"Uh-huh," Lizzie said, looking very bored.

"Maybe you'd like to get involved in some of those activities," Jana added hopefully.

"Yeah, right," Lizzie said sarcastically. "Like, I'd really like to be in a school play." She made a gagging noise.

"It was just a suggestion," Jana said in a small voice. "Maybe you'll like your afternoon classes better, Lizzie."

Lizzie sat back in her chair and gazed at Jana for a moment. "Would you do me a favor, Jana?"

"Sure," Jana said, eager to help.

"Would you call me Liz instead of Lizzie?"

"Oh, sure, okay," Jana said.

Lizzie nodded and folded her arms across her chest. "Just my good friends call me Lizzie."

CHAPTER

4

"She was angry and mean all day!" Jana said. "She thought school was boring. She didn't like our teachers. She said I talked too much. And *then* she asked me to call her Liz instead of Lizzie."

"Why?" her mother asked, taking the casserole out of the oven. "What's wrong with Lizzie?"

Jana raised her eyebrows. "Only her *good friends* call her Lizzie," Jana said. "*Obviously* she has no intention of ever letting me be a good friend."

Jana's stepfather, Pink, had just finished setting the table. He strolled over to Jana and put his arm around her shoulder.

"The girl sounds as if she's built a wall around herself," he said. "By telling you that only her

27

friends call her Lizzie, she's saying that she wants to keep you at a distance."

"Exactly," Jana said, shrugging to show her exasperation. "That's the trouble, but why would she want to do that? Doesn't she want to make new friends?"

"Maybe she feels insecure," her mother said. "The name 'Lizzie' sounds a little younger, a little more vulnerable than 'Liz,' which sounds more like a mature, independent young woman. Maybe she feels a little threatened by her new situation and wants to be called by a more sophisticated name."

"Maybe," Jana grumbled, but she wasn't convinced. Maybe Liz was just a crabby person who got her kicks by hurting other people's feelings.

"Dinner's ready," her mother called.

The three squeezed into their places at the kitchen table.

"Where does Liz live?" Pink asked.

"At a shelter for the homeless—Phoenix House," Jana said.

Pink smiled. "Good name," he said.

Jana frowned, trying to understand. "Phoenix? You mean, the city in Arizona?"

"Well, originally the name came from mythology," Pink said, spooning a helping of casserole onto his plate. "A phoenix was a bird. Only one phoenix existed at a time," he went on. "It lived a very long time, and at the end of its life, it burned itself in a funeral pyre."

"That's sad," Jana said, putting down her fork.

"No, not really," said Pink. "Because another phoenix rose up in its place, filled with youth and beauty. Because of its rebirth, the phoenix has come to represent starting life over with renewed strength and determination."

"I'm impressed, Pink," Jana's mother said, grinning. "I didn't know you knew Greek mythology."

"My high-school English teacher, Mrs. Mortimer, gets the credit. She pounded all that stuff into our heads during my junior year."

"Say, I have an idea," her mother said. "Why not invite Lizzie—excuse me, *Liz*—over for dinner on Saturday?"

Jana thought a moment and then nodded. "Yeah, okay," she said. "It's worth a try, anyway. Maybe she'll see that I'm not so awful, and she'll loosen up a little."

"I'll fix chicken and dumplings and green beans—"

"Oooh, invite her to come every night," Pink teased. "If we get to eat like that when she comes, I like her already."

Jana's mother laughed.

"Thanks, Mom," Jana said. "I'll ask her tomorrow at school."

"She'll need to check with her mother," Mrs. Pinkerton said. "Tell her we can pick her up if she needs a ride."

"I can't wait to invite her," Jana said. "I hope she says yes."

After supper Jana helped with the dishes and then

went to her room. She had just opened her lit book when the phone rang.

"Jana, it's for you!" Pink called from the living room.

"Thanks, Pink, I'll take it in your bedroom," Jana called back. She hurried into her parents' bedroom and picked up the receiver.

"Hello?"

"Hi, Jana. It's Randy."

Jana's heart fluttered a little at the sound of Randy's voice. He'd had that effect on her ever since the fourth grade. Jana had noticed lots of other nice, cute boys in school, but none of them could ever compete with Randy.

"Hi, Randy," she said softly.

"How did the first day go with the new girl?"

"Awful," Jana confessed. "She's . . . well, she's not one of the friendliest people I've ever met, let's put it that way."

"Gosh, that's too bad," Randy said. "What's her problem?"

"Mom thinks maybe she feels a little threatened," said Jana. "I suppose because she's new. I'm going to invite her over for dinner Saturday night and see if that helps."

"Good idea," Randy said. "Hey, I've missed seeing you around this week. Want to meet me at Bumpers tomorrow after school?"

"Great! I'd love to."

"Super," said Randy. "See you then."

Jana nearly floated back to her room. She was going to see Randy tomorrow after school, and she was going to invite Liz for dinner on Saturday. She just knew that her mom and Pink could help win Liz over, no matter how hard Liz might try to resist.

Maybe things were looking up.

"Liz, these are my closest friends in the world," Jana said proudly the next day during lunch period. She hadn't gotten up the nerve yet to ask Liz to her house on Saturday, and now Jana and Liz stood with their trays next to the table where The Fabulous Five always sat. Liz was wearing the same pair of jeans, plaid shirt, and jacket that she had worn yesterday. "This is Beth Barry, Katie Shannon, Christie Winchell, and Melanie Edwards," Jana went on. "The five of us make up The Fabulous Five."

"Oh, yeah?" Liz mumbled. "What's so fabulous about you guys?"

Jana winced inwardly. Why did Liz act this way? She wanted her friends to like Liz and help her feel at home. But how could they when Liz behaved like a jerk?

There was an awkward silence for a moment. Melanie cleared her throat and glanced nervously from Beth to Katie to Jana, obviously hoping someone would say something helpful.

"Sit down," Beth offered, and moved her tray over to give Liz room. Melanie sighed loudly with relief, and Jana seated herself across from Liz.

"It's very nice to have you here at Wakeman, Liz," Melanie said. Jana thought she sounded as if she were being dutifully polite, saying something she didn't mean.

Liz rolled her eyes. "Uh-huh," she said, looking bored.

"No, it really is," Beth insisted. "It's always great to meet new people." Around the table, the others nodded eagerly.

"Liz, if you need help getting caught up in math, the person to ask for help is Christie," Jana said. "She's really a whiz."

"Well, I don't know that I'm a whiz, but I'd be happy to help you," Christie said sincerely.

Liz nodded but didn't say anything. She picked up the peanut butter sandwich in front of her and took a tiny bite.

"And I'm pretty good in English," Jana said.

Still no response from Liz.

"What do you like to do?" Melanie asked Liz. "I mean, what are your hobbies?"

Liz glanced at Melanie and then at Jana and finally at the table. She looks scared, thought Jana.

"I don't have any hobbies," Liz mumbled. Jana could barely hear her.

"What?" Melanie asked.

"*I said, I don't have any hobbies! You deaf, or what?*" Liz shouted, her eyes filling with tears. She grabbed her books from the floor, stood up, and ran out of the cafeteria.

"What did I say?" cried Melanie, looking bewildered.

"Mel," Jana said gently, "Liz lives in a shelter for the homeless, remember? The last thing on her mind is a hobby."

Melanie gulped and blinked back tears of her own. "I'm sorry," she said. "I wasn't thinking."

"That's okay, Mel," Katie said. "I have a feeling that Liz is pretty tough. I don't think your question killed her. We'll just have to be more thoughtful about what she's going through and try to ask the *right* questions from now on."

"She sure isn't easy to get to know," Jana said, sighing. She got up and collected her own books. "I just wish I knew the right way to handle her."

"Why don't you talk to some of the other kids who're helping homeless students," Beth suggested. "Maybe they're having the same problems."

"Good idea," Jana said. "I'll call Whitney tonight. Excuse me now, guys, I think I'd better see if I can find Liz."

Jana left the table and hurried out into the hall. Miss Dickinson, her English teacher, was walking toward her with an armload of books.

"Miss Dickinson," Jana said, "have you seen Liz Flagg?"

"Yes," said the teacher. "She came running this way. I was about to ask her to slow down, but she looked so upset, I decided to let it go. I think she may have ducked into the girls' bathroom at the end of the hall."

"Thanks," Jana said, and sped off in that direction.

She found Liz in the last stall at the back of the restroom. She recognized the old, worn sneakers under the door.

"Liz?" she called softly.

There was no answer.

"Liz, Melanie didn't mean to hurt you or make you mad," Jana said. "She feels really bad that she said the wrong thing. Won't you come out so I can talk to you?"

"Go away," Liz said. "I don't want to talk to you."

Jana sighed. "Liz, we just want to be your friends. Honest."

"I don't need any friends," she said.

Jana tried to think of what she could say to make Liz feel better, but then she considered the possibility that maybe Liz really *didn't* want to have friends at Wakeman.

"Okay," Jana said. "If that's what you want."

She turned and walked out of the restroom, hoping that Liz might call her back. But she didn't.

Jana had planned to talk to Liz during one of their afternoon classes. She wanted to reassure Liz that she was liked and wanted at Wakeman. And she wanted to invite her to have dinner with her family on Saturday.

She didn't get the chance, though, because Liz didn't show up at any of her classes for the rest of the day.

CHAPTER

5

"This is it, this is it!" Melanie's eyes grew large with excitement. "This is the fourth day of the true love test! With everything that went on at lunch, I nearly forgot!"

Jana and Beth had arrived at Bumpers right after school. Melanie, Christie, and Katie had come shortly afterward. Since Randy hadn't gotten there yet, Jana was sitting with The Fabulous Five in a booth, positioned so that she could see him when he walked in the door.

"So, what happens on the fourth day?" Beth asked. "I've forgotten already."

"If you'd taken the test when I offered it to you, you'd remember, but since you didn't, I'll explain it again. On the fourth day, you drink a glass of water,

35

then say your favorite guy's name," Melanie explained patiently.

"Uh-huh," said Christie. "Then what?"

"Within four days, he'll ask you out or say he likes you," Melanie said dreamily. "Isn't that romantic?"

"Okay, Mel, now's the time," Beth said. "I'll ask for a glass of water."

She scooted out of the booth and hurried up to the soda fountain. Within half a minute, she returned with a cup of ice water.

Melanie glanced into the cup, and a frown creased her forehead.

"What's wrong?" Katie asked.

"Well, there's ice in here," Melanie said slowly. "The test didn't say anything about ice."

"I'm sure it doesn't make any difference," Jana said, smiling. "A glass of water is a glass of water."

Melanie frowned again. "Yeah, and that's another thing. This container isn't made of glass either. It's a paper cup," she said. "Wow, I hope I don't mess this up. What if it doesn't work because it's ice water in a cup, instead of just plain water in a glass?"

"Don't worry about it," Katie said. "If the crazy thing works *anyway*, it'll be a miracle."

"No," Melanie said worriedly. "I'd better do it right. Excuse me, Beth, but I think I'll ask if they have a glass and I'll dump the ice out."

"Oh, brother," Katie said with a sigh.

"Be right back. Don't go away!" said Melanie, flushed with anticipation.

"She's having fun," said Jana. "Let's play along."

Melanie returned in a minute, holding up a small water glass. "And no ice," she said. She clutched the glass with both hands and stared upward dramatically.

"Now is the time," she whispered, her eyes sparkling. "Now I drink the water and say the name of the boy who will become my own true love!"

"Whose name are you going to say?" Beth interrupted.

"Keep your shirt on, Beth," Melanie said impatiently. "I'm trying to create a mood here."

"Oh, sorry," Beth said. "Go on."

"First, I drink—" Melanie said. She lifted the glass slowly to her lips and drank the liquid.

Suddenly Richie Corrierro came out of nowhere. He had a frog wriggling in his hand, and he held it up in front of Melanie's face. "Hey, Melanie!" he cried, laughing. "Kiss it! It's a prince!"

Melanie screamed and almost dropped the empty water glass, and Richie doubled over with laughter. Then he dangled the frog by a back leg and shouted through his laughter, "Ha, ha. It's only rubber!"

"RICHIE CORRIERRO! You're the most disgusting—"

Suddenly she stopped and slapped a hand over her mouth.

"Oh, no! What have I done!" she gasped, her eyes wide with horror.

"You said, 'Richie Corrierro!'" Jana said. "Does that mean—"

"That means *he'll* become my one true love!" Melanie wailed, sinking into the booth as her knees gave way. "Richie Corrierro! Yuck! Yuck! Yuck! This can't be happening. It just *can't*!" She put her hands over her face.

"Don't worry, Mel," Katie said. "This test is a fake, anyway. People don't fall in love after taking a test and drinking a glass of water—"

"And I did everything right, too!" moaned Melanie, completely ignoring Katie. "The container made of glass and no ice! I did everything *perfectly*! I'm doomed, doomed!"

"No, you're not," Beth said. "You can get almost any boy you want by being nice, and—"

"I was going to say Shane Arrington's name!" Melanie wailed. "If I'd done it right, I'd be waiting for Shane's call asking me out. He might have said he *liked* me! But no, now that's impossible. *Now* when I get that phone call, it'll be from dumb, stupid Richie Corrierro. I'd even rather have said the name of Shane's iguana, *Igor*! *Yeckh!* I can't stand it!"

Jana put a hand on Melanie's shoulder. "Mel, don't worry. If Richie calls, just say no and then be super nice to the guys you really like. The test won't matter."

"You can't change fate," Melanie said despondently. "What happened here this afternoon was fate. I know, because the test worked for my cousin."

"What happened here this afternoon was dumb," said Beth. "Really, Mel, I can't believe you're taking this so seriously."

Melanie glanced over Beth's shoulder and then her eyes grew wide. "It's Shane!" she gasped. "Shane just walked into Bumpers!"

"Why don't you go over and say hi?" asked Jana.

"But, I can't—"

"Go ahead," Jana insisted, gently nudging Melanie toward the edge of the booth. "Put the love test to the *ultimate* test. Go talk to Shane and see what happens."

Melanie bit her lower lip and gave Jana a wary look. Then she sighed shakily and said, "Okay. Here goes."

Jana crossed her fingers behind her back and watched Melanie walk slowly toward Shane.

"Uh-oh! Look who's coming toward Shane from the other direction," said Katie.

All four girls grabbed one another's hands and held their breath as Laura McCall sauntered over to Shane. She was far enough ahead of Melanie to reach him while Melanie was still several steps away. Then Laura put a hand on Shane's arm and whispered something to him.

Jana watched in horror as the two of them talked and giggled together while Melanie stood, staring at them, from the middle of the floor. Suddenly she

whirled around and stomped back to The Fabulous
Five's booth, tears spurting into her eyes.

"See? I told you the test works," she said between
sobs. "I just proved it!"

"But, Mel—" Jana started to protest.

"You saw it," Melanie cried. "Stupid, crummy
Laura McCall came up and started flirting her head
off with Shane, and he just flirted right back and
ignored me completely!"

"How could he ignore you?" asked Christie,
frowning. "You weren't over there more than five
seconds."

"Yeah," added Katie. "He probably didn't even
know you were there."

"He didn't know I was there because of the love
test! Don't you understand? I'm fated to have a
crummy love life for the next four years!" Melanie
jumped to her feet. "I'm going home. This is the
worst day of my entire life!"

"Mel!" cried Jana, grabbing Melanie's sleeve.
"Stay here. You know you'll feel better if you're with
your friends."

"Right," said Beth. "Give him a second chance."

"Are you kidding?" huffed Melanie. "And humili-
ate myself two times in one afternoon? No way!"

"But don't you see what you're doing?" asked
Christie. "You're *making* that stupid test work! You
didn't give Shane a chance when Laura walked over.
She isn't with him now, but now you won't even talk
to *him*."

"He's looking this way," Jana said, trying to talk without moving her lips so that he wouldn't be able to tell what she was saying. "Melanie! Turn around and smile at him."

Melanie shot up straight as a poker. "Where is he?"

"Over there," Jana said, nodding slightly in Shane's direction.

Melanie took a deep breath and pasted a big smile on her face before swinging around to look toward Shane. But just then, he looked away and started talking with friends.

"You didn't look fast enough," Jana insisted when she saw the crushed expression on Melanie's face.

"Oh, yeah? Well, I give up! I'm going home!" She swept her books into her arms and stormed out of Bumpers.

CHAPTER

6

*M*elanie had scarcely gotten out the door when Randy walked into Bumpers. Jana waved him over.

"Hi," he said to everyone in the booth. "Where's Melanie?"

There was total silence for a moment, and then Jana said, "She was here, but she had to get home. Big test Monday or something."

She didn't look at any of the other members of The Fabulous Five when she said that. She hated to lie, but Melanie would absolutely die if any boy ever found out about her love test. Even Randy, Jana thought with a sigh, who is the kindest and most sensitive boy who ever lived.

"Earth to Jana. Earth to Jana," said Randy, bringing her back to reality. He was grinning, and Jana grinned back, knowing how he loved to tease her. "Want to walk home?" he asked.

"Sure," Jana said, glad to get some time alone with him. "I'm ready now. Let's go."

Jana and Randy said good-bye to the girls and headed for the door. Just then, Lee Brophy, a blond eighth-grade girl, walked in. She held up her hand in a greeting.

"Hi, Jana," she said. "I've seen you with that homeless girl at school." Lee wrinkled her nose when she said "homeless" as if the word itself had a bad odor. "How's that working out, anyway?"

Jana winced at Lee's haughty expression. "Well," she said, trying to phrase her answer carefully, "she's trying to get used to Wacko. It's quite an adjustment for her."

The girl rolled her eyes. "Hmph. I certainly hope she's grateful that you're spending so much time with her."

"Oh, I don't know—" Jana began, but Lee interrupted her.

"I suppose she can't help how her parents live their lives, but—well, I just don't have much sympathy for those people."

Little explosions went off in Jana's brain. "What do you mean?" she demanded.

"What I mean is, why don't her parents get jobs?" said Lee, narrowing her eyes. "Then they could live in an apartment instead of a homeless shelter where the taxpayers have to feed them. I just don't understand people like that—people who want handouts instead of standing on their own two feet. Talk about lazy."

Jana bristled. She couldn't stand to hear Lee talk this way, but she didn't exactly know how to answer, either.

"Well, I don't know that much about Liz," Jana began. "But there are a lot of people who've had some bad luck through no fault of their own. They're not lazy at all, but they need help, and they can get it at the shelter. And in the meantime, they can look for work. I'm sure everything is going to work out just fine for Liz in time."

"Oh, come on, Jana, get real," said Lee. "Those people aren't like us."

"What do you mean?" Jana asked warily. She didn't like the smirk on Lee's face.

"Well, for one thing," Lee said with an air of superiority, "her hair is always a greasy mess. I mean, doesn't she have any pride? How tough is it to wash your hair, even at a shelter?"

Jana stared at Lee for a moment, unable to say anything. Lee gave Jana a small, tight smile of triumph and walked away.

Randy put his arm around Jana and steered her out the door. "Hey, don't let her get to you," he said gently. "You knew when you started this that not everyone would understand."

Jana nodded. He was right, of course, but something else was bothering her. "Randy, can I tell you a secret?"

Randy stopped in the middle of the sidewalk and looked at her with astonishment. "Of course," he said. "I thought you knew that."

"I do," Jana said with an embarrassed little laugh. "It's just that . . . well . . . I don't know exactly how to say it."

"Try," Randy said softly.

Jana swallowed hard. "Lee isn't the only one who doesn't totally understand," she began. "Sometimes I don't either."

She shifted from one foot to the other while Randy stood waiting patiently beside her. "What Lee said about Liz's hair always being a greasy mess is true," she went on. "I try not to let it bother me, and it makes me feel awfully guilty to say it out loud, but I've wondered the same thing Lee did. Doesn't Liz have any pride? I mean, she always looks so grubby. And she refuses to take off that ratty-looking red down jacket. She wears it all the time, instead of putting it in her locker like everyone else. If she washed her hair and tried to look a little neater, kids might be more interested in getting to know her."

Randy sighed. "I've noticed that, too. But that's not the only problem she's giving you, is it?"

Jana sighed. "Well, I don't think she's giving me problems on purpose. It's just that she acts as if she doesn't want anyone to get close to her. She's really unhappy, and she doesn't even try to be nice to other people. Sometimes I wonder if she lets her hair stay greasy on purpose, just to gross people out and keep them away."

"Wow, that sounds tough," Randy said. "I wish I could think of something that would help." Then he squeezed her hand. "But she's crazy if she doesn't want to be *your* friend. She doesn't know how lucky she is."

Jana felt a warm glow in her chest. Randy always knew just the right thing to say. She snuggled close as they walked along.

"Thanks, Randy," she said. "I really needed that."

They walked on a few minutes silently.

"So what's your next move with Liz?" asked Randy.

"I think I'll call Whitney Larkin tonight," she said. "Maybe her new partner is acting the same way that Liz is. Maybe she'll have some suggestions. You know, things that she tried that worked."

"Good idea," said Randy. "Couldn't hurt, anyway. And Jana," he added thoughtfully, "just be yourself. Nobody—not even Liz—could ask for more than that."

Jana grinned and kissed him quickly on the cheek.

Randy stopped right in the middle of the sidewalk and with a finger under her chin, tilted her face up to his.

"We can do better than that," he said.

He kissed her softly, and for that moment, Jana forgot all about her troubles with Liz, Melanie's love test, and everything else in her life. For that moment, it was just her and Randy. And she felt wonderful.

"Hello?" Whitney answered the phone. There was classical music playing in the background.

"Whitney? This is Jana Morgan."

"Oh, hi, Jana," Whitney said. "Just a minute. Let me turn down the CD player."

Jana heard Whitney set the receiver down and walk away from the phone. In a moment, the music was shut off, and the footsteps returned.

"Now I can hear you," Whitney said. "What's up?"

"Whitney, how are things going with your new student?" Jana asked.

Whitney's voice dropped. "Oh." Her first word told Jana what she wanted to know. She was having problems, too.

"Well," Whitney continued, "it hasn't been the way I thought it would be. Leslie is really . . . well, she's really different."

"In what way?" asked Jana.

"She hardly talks to me at all," Whitney said. "In fact, she hasn't said more than five words to me since she started school this week. And I'm with her everyday."

"Well," Jana said, "I sometimes wish Liz *wouldn't* talk to me. When she does, she's really mean."

"Right," said Whitney. "What's with them, anyway?"

"Maybe they feel threatened," Jana said, remembering what her mother had told her.

"About what?" Whitney asked.

Jana sighed. "I'm not sure. I guess they've been hurt a lot by their experiences, and they're embarrassed that they're living in the shelter. Maybe they're so sure that nobody will understand that they won't even let us try. I think Liz is that way. The more I *try* to help her, the nastier she gets."

"You're probably right," said Whitney. "Have you been getting . . . comments from other kids?"

"You mean like, why don't their parents get jobs?" asked Jana.

"Right," said Whitney. "Even my own father said something like that. And two of my best friends don't even want to meet Leslie. They say that if she won't talk to *me*, why bother trying to make friends with her."

"Can I ask you something else? Something private?" Jana asked softly.

"Sure."

"Sometimes do you feel . . . funny . . . about her, too? I mean, I really want to help Liz and everything, but I can't help thinking that if she really wanted to fit in at Wacko, she'd try harder. She'd *let* me help her instead of always pushing me away."

Jana heard Whitney breathe a sigh of relief. "Exactly," she whispered. "They act as if they don't want us to help them. That's weird, if you ask me."

"Maybe we should talk to Mrs. Brenner," said Jana. "She said we could come to her if we needed help."

"And we do," agreed Whitney. "Let's go see her before school on Monday. Maybe she'll know what to do. Nothing else has worked."

"Great," said Jana. "I'll see you Monday morning then, right after the first bell. Let's hope this helps," she added before hanging up.

CHAPTER

7

"Could we talk to you a minute, Mrs. Brenner?" Jana asked.

Jana had tried all weekend to keep Liz out of her mind. She had worked on homework, gone out to dinner with her mother and Pink, and talked on the phone with both Randy and Beth. But Liz was never far from her thoughts. As soon as her homework was done or she had put down the receiver, her mind was flooded again with images of Liz and her mother trying to get by without a home. But now the weekend was over, and she and Whitney stood in the counselor's office.

"Of course, girls," Mrs. Brenner said. "Have a seat."

There were two molded plastic chairs opposite

Mrs. Brenner's desk, and the girls sat down in them.

"What can I do for you?" Mrs. Brenner asked pleasantly.

Jana and Whitney exchanged glances before Jana spoke. "We're having trouble with the girls we're paired with."

"What kind of trouble?" asked Mrs. Brenner.

"Liz seems so angry all the time," answered Jana. "She acts as if she doesn't want any friends. And she's mean."

Whitney spoke up. "So is Leslie. I mean, she doesn't even talk to me, and she couldn't care less about anything going on at school."

Mrs. Brenner listened and nodded while the girls talked. "This kind of behavior is to be expected."

"Really?" asked Jana. "Why?"

"Well, I'm sure it's important for both of you to feel that *you* fit in," said Mrs. Brenner. "Right?"

Jana thought about how much she counted on the rest of The Fabulous Five to give her support and make her feel secure. "Sure," she said.

"Right," Whitney admitted. "I had a hard time earlier in the year because I skipped a grade."

"Well, the same is true for the homeless kids," Mrs. Brenner said. "They're having a hard time fitting in."

"We know that," Jana insisted. "That's why we wanted to help them out in the first place."

"And they don't try to be friends with anybody,"

said Whitney. "They act as if they don't *want* friends."

"Oh, I assure you they do," Mrs. Brenner said. "But they look at you two girls—and all the other kids—who *do* have homes, and they feel ashamed about living in a shelter."

"I haven't even brought up the subject of living in a shelter," said Jana.

"But Liz knows you are aware that she lives in Phoenix House," Mrs. Brenner explained. "That's enough."

"So what can we do?" asked Whitney. "Just being nice doesn't seem to help."

"How would you feel about talking with the girls about their situations?"

"Nervous," admitted Whitney.

"Wouldn't that be prying?" asked Jana. "Especially if they're ashamed about living in the shelter."

Mrs. Brenner sighed. "Perhaps not, particularly if you understand the types of problems these kids have been facing. You see, most of them haven't been to school for a long time because their parents are afraid their children will be taken away from them."

"By whom?" asked Jana.

"The police, social workers, hospital personnel," Mrs. Brenner said. "Parents *know* they aren't providing adequately for their kids if the family is living in an abandoned house or in a car. And they know that welfare workers can take their children away and place them in foster homes. So many parents don't *try* to get their children into schools. They're afraid, and they want to keep the family together. Many times, their children are all they have."

Jana stared at the floor. "That's so sad."

"Yes, it is," said Mrs. Brenner. "And without an education, these kids won't be any better off when they grow up. We're hoping that this program works so that other homeless parents will know that they can send their children to school without being afraid of losing them. In school, the kids not only get a good education, but they also get a hot lunch every day and breakfast, too, if they want it."

"Mrs. Brenner," said Jana, "I met Liz's mother that first day. What about her father?"

"She never knew her father," Mrs. Brenner said softly. "He left shortly after Liz was born. Mrs. Flagg and Liz lived in a trailer in another city for the past several years. Then Mrs. Flagg lost her job when there were cutbacks at the factory where she worked, and a week later, their trailer was destroyed by fire."

"Wow," whispered Jana. "I had no idea Liz had been through so much."

Mrs. Brenner turned to Whitney. "Leslie's mother lived with her two girls in a car for a month before she got help at Phoenix House. She's looking for another job now. The adults at Phoenix House have to be actively looking for work in order to stay there. So you see what an important job you girls are doing."

Jana nodded. She really did understand. And she wanted to do a *good* job. She just wished she could like Liz and that Liz would try harder to be liked.

"We must be careful not to judge other people," said Mrs. Brenner, as if she had read Jana's mind. "Most of us haven't had to deal with the problems these homeless people have faced."

"So you think we should talk to them about Phoenix House?" Jana asked.

"Well, I wouldn't go charging into your first period class and bombard them with questions about the shelter," Mrs. Brenner replied with a little smile. "But don't avoid the issue, either. For instance, Jana, if Liz has trouble with a particular homework assignment, you might ask her how she gets her studying done at the shelter. Then offer to help or have her over to your house to study. You might even offer to go with her to the library."

"That's a good idea," said Jana.

"I'm glad we talked to Mrs. Brenner," Whitney said as they walked out into the hall after the meeting. "I think maybe I understand just a little better."

"Me, too," Jana said.

Just then, a commotion at the end of the hall drew their attention.

"What's going on down there?" Jana asked, frowning.

Whitney gasped. "It's a fight!"

"Who's fighting?" asked Jana as they moved

closer. She peered into the crowd that was gathering, hoping that it was no one she knew.

"I don't know," Whitney said. "Two guys."

The crowd of students surrounding the boys blocked their view. Everyone looked upset at what was going on.

"Oh, grow up, you guys!" somebody yelled.

"Come on, stop it!" someone else called out.

Just then, Mr. Bell and Mr. Dracovitch came running down the hall, and after a brief struggle with the boys, they managed to separate them.

Jana and Whitney stood on their toes, trying to see who had been fighting.

"Can you see?" Whitney asked Jana. "I still don't know who it is."

Before Jana could reply, the boy standing in front of Whitney turned around and sneered. "Who do you *think*? One of the guys from Phoenix House is picking on one of our guys. I just knew there'd be trouble if we let those kids come into our school!"

CHAPTER

8

*J*ana felt sick. All morning she heard kids talking about the fight between the boy from Phoenix House and an eighth-grader she didn't know. And most of the talk was that the kids from Phoenix House were nothing but trouble.

It wasn't fair, she thought. Just because a boy from the homeless shelter was involved in a fight, why did everyone lump all the homeless kids together as troublemakers?

Liz was back, but she avoided Jana before the morning bell and during first-period history. Just before class ended Mr. Naset announced that a test on the British colonists in America would be given on Wednesday. Jana decided to try to talk to Liz about the test.

She caught up with Liz at lunchtime just inside the cafeteria. Liz's hair hung in stringy clumps, as usual, and she wore her ratty-looking red down jacket. Jana tried her best to ignore Liz's appearance and concentrate on what she wanted to say.

"Mr. Naset's tests are usually pretty hard. Would you like to study together? I can give you some tips about the kind of questions he asks."

"No," Liz said, not even breaking her stride.

Jana took a deep breath and tried to fight down her rising frustration. She was determined to make this work.

Jana and her friends went through the lunch line with Liz in front of them and picked up their food. Liz walked to a table across the cafeteria from The Fabulous Five's table and sat down. Jana followed and sat down with her.

"The test will be on some of the stuff we covered before you came to Wakeman," Jana said. "Would you like to borrow my notes?"

Liz shook her head and then gazed into space over Jana's left shoulder.

Jana didn't know whether this was the right time to talk about the shelter, but she decided she sure couldn't lose anything. Liz was just as withdrawn and unfriendly as she had been on the first day.

"Is it hard to study at Phoenix House?" Jana asked.

Liz looked at her sharply and, at first, didn't say

anything. Finally, she nodded slightly. "Yeah," she said softly. "The place is pretty crazy."

"Crazy, how?" Jana asked, encouraged.

Liz shrugged. "Babies crying, little kids running around, everybody's talking. It's not very quiet, that's all."

"Would you like to come over and study with me for the test? My mom and step-dad are always quiet when I need to study."

Liz gazed at Jana for a moment, but Jana could not read her expression.

"Well, maybe," she said slowly.

Jana couldn't believe what she had just heard, but she was careful not to let her excitement show. "Great. How about tomorrow night after supper?" She decided not to push it by asking Liz to eat over.

Liz shrugged. "Okay," she said without enthusiasm.

"How about seven o'clock?" Jana asked. "We could pick you up—"

"No," said Liz. "Where do you live?"

Jana gave Liz the address.

"I'll walk," Liz said.

"Well, okay," Jana said. "But you probably shouldn't walk back after we're finished. It'll be dark. Mom or Pink could drop you off."

Liz thought that over for a moment. "Okay," she said slowly, sounding almost pleased. "I guess that would be okay."

Jana handed Liz her notebook. "Go ahead and

copy the stuff we covered before you came. Then
tomorrow night we'll study all of the material."

To Jana's relief, Liz took the notebook. Maybe,
just maybe, this was going to work.

Jana smiled. "Great. We'll make popcorn. It'll be
fun."

Liz shrugged, and Jana saw that the wall surrounding Liz that had briefly been opened in one
little spot now stood as high and strong as ever.

"Oh, no! Don't look now," said Melanie, wrinkling
her nose and ducking her head. "Here comes Richie
Corrierro. *Beth, I said, DON'T LOOK!*"

Jana, Melanie, and Beth stood in front of Jana's
locker after school.

"Quick, open your locker, Jana!" Melanie whispered.

Jana spun her combination lock around several
times and flung open the door. Melanie whipped out
her brush and pretended to fix her hair while she
looked in the mirror hanging on the inside of the
door.

"Talk. Act natural. We're having a conversation,"
Melanie whispered. "I don't want Richie to stop
here and ask me out!"

"So—" Beth said. "Uh, Jana, how is the project
for homeless kids going?"

"Uh, uh, pretty well," Jana said. "In fact, Liz and
I are studying together tomorrow night."

"That's nice," Melanie said in a loud voice as Richie walked nearer. "Don't you think that's nice, Beth?"

"Uh, sure, Mel," Beth said.

"Well, I've just been so ve-ry busy," Melanie said in an even louder voice. "I haven't had time for going out or anything fun! You see, my aunt is here from out of town—"

Beth looked at Jana and rolled her eyes.

"—and we've spent day and night showing her around. Oh, and then there's my homework—"

Beth tapped Melanie on the shoulder.

"—there's that history test coming up this week and my parents have really been cracking down on me to study—"

"Mel," Beth said.

"—and I have my chores at home to do—"

"Mel, he's gone," Beth said.

"—emptying the wastebaskets and taking out the garbage—"

"Mel," Beth insisted. "Richie walked right by you and didn't say a word. You can stop now."

"—and I always have to wash the dish—" She stopped. "He's gone?"

"Yeah," said Beth. "He walked right by."

"He may have walked by," Melanie said, "but I saw the look on his face when he was coming down the hall. He looked at me, and it's obvious."

"What's obvious?" asked Jana.

"He wants me! Couldn't you tell? He wants us to

go out!" Melanie wailed. "That love test has ruined my life!"

"But, Melanie," Jana said gently, "I was watching Richie, and he didn't even look over here when he went by."

"That's because I was talking about how *busy* I was!" Melanie huffed. "He knew I'd turn him down and he didn't want to be humiliated, so he kept on walking!"

"Oh, brother," Beth muttered.

"What am I going to do?" asked Melanie. "I can't always pretend to be very, very busy, or the word will get out that I'm too busy to date. Then even if some guy was brave enough and willing to fight fate to ask me out, he wouldn't because he'd think I wouldn't be available anyway!"

"Did you get all that?" Beth asked Jana.

"I think so," said Jana, trying not to smile. "Look, Melanie, you trust me, don't you?"

"Well, sure, Jana," Melanie said. "You're one of my best friends."

"Well then, hear me out," Jana said. "I know you think the love test is doing all these things to you, making Richie love you and turning all other boys against you, but it doesn't make sense. Love doesn't work that way."

"Jana," Melanie said very patiently, "I know that you know a lot about boys, but let me say as kindly as I can that—as smart and knowledgeable and perceptive as you are about boys—you don't know *diddly* about fate."

"What?"

"It's fate, plain and simple," Melanie said sadly. "My life is over where boys are concerned, for at least four years. But I'll just have to get through it the best I can. I'll just have to concentrate on how wonderful my life will be when I'm a junior in high school and this curse has passed."

"That's crazy, Melanie!" Beth exploded. "That's idiotic! There's no power in that dumb test, except for the power that you give it!"

"Power," Melanie murmured, staring into space. "Beth, that's it!"

Beth frowned and shook her head. "What's it?"

"If the test has power over my love life, maybe I can find an *antidote* to it!" Melanie exclaimed happily.

"What?" whispered Beth, frowning and shaking her head even harder.

"An antidote!" Melanie repeated. "Maybe I can break the spell somehow! I'm going to the library on my way home. Maybe I can find something that will stop the spell from working."

Jana sighed as she exchanged glances with Beth.

"Okay, Mel," Jana said. "Suit yourself. But I think you're wasting your time."

"You don't think I'll find a spell-breaker?" Melanie asked anxiously.

"I don't think there's a spell to break," Jana said. "But I think you have your mind already made up."

"Right!" Melanie said enthusiastically. "Either of you want to come with me?"

"No, thanks," said Jana.

"No, Mel," Beth said. "I have a lot of homework."

"Okay, I'll see you guys later," Melanie said. "I just know I'll find something to break this spell." She turned and walked several steps toward the front door, then stopped and whirled around with a big grin on her face. "When you see me again, I'll be a *free woman*!"

CHAPTER

9

*J*ana sat on the living room couch and waited for the doorbell to ring. It was 7:07, and already she was wondering if Liz might not show up.

Pink strolled into the room. "Just waiting?" he asked.

"Mm-hmm," Jana said. "She said she'd come at seven."

"She'll probably be here any minute."

"Maybe," Jana said. "But then again, maybe she decided not to stick her neck out."

Pink sat down on the couch beside her. "What do you mean?" he asked.

"Well, I've been thinking about this," Jana said. "Coming here is a big step for Liz. She's taking a risk by letting me spend a little time with her, by letting you drive her back to the shelter. If she's embarrassed about being homeless, coming here to our home is probably tough for her."

Pink nodded. "I think you're right."

"So maybe she decided just to skip it, to stay safe and not take the risk," said Jana.

"You know," Pink said with a grin, "you're a pretty smart girl. No, maybe *perceptive* is a better word here."

"How about smart *and* perceptive?" Jana teased.

"Now you're talking," Pink said, squeezing her shoulder.

Just then the doorbell rang, and Jana's stomach did a flip-flop. "She's here! She really came!" Jana whispered.

"You open the door," Pink whispered back. "I'll get lost."

"Thanks," said Jana. Pink disappeared down the hall to the master bedroom.

Jana hurried to the door and pulled it open. "Hi, Liz," she said. "Come on in."

Liz was wearing blue jeans, a blue cotton blouse, and, as usual, her red down jacket. She carried two notebooks and her school textbook.

"Hi," she said just above a whisper.

She isn't smiling and she looks a little nervous, Jana thought. She wondered briefly if she should ask to take Liz's jacket, but decided against it. If Liz wanted to take it off, she would.

Jana ushered her into the living room. Liz stood in

the middle of the floor and looked around at the dining room table with its silk-flower centerpiece, at the homey kitchen around the corner, at the comfortable furniture in the living room and the wall covered with photographs of Jana's family. She didn't speak.

"I thought we could study right here," Jana said. "Mom and Pink are going to watch TV in their bedroom, so we won't be in the way, and my room is really too small for us both to study there."

I'm talking too much and too fast again, Jana thought. Taking a deep breath, she gestured to the couch. "Have a seat."

Liz walked over to the couch and sat down, and Jana followed. Liz's gold earrings caught the light from the lamp on the end table and shone brightly.

Jana leaned toward Liz. "Those are beautiful earrings. I noticed them at school."

"Thanks," Liz said. There was a little pause, and she touched the left earring gently. "They belonged to my grandmother. They're real gold."

"I wish I had a pair like them," Jana said. "They're gorgeous."

Liz looked off into space. "My grandmother died three years ago. I used to live with her some of the time."

"Really?" Jana said, both surprised and delighted that Liz had lowered that wall a little to talk about her life. "Where did you live?"

Abruptly, the wall was snapped back into place. "Out of state," Liz snapped, and looked away.

"Oh," said Jana, swallowing hard. "Well, I guess we'd better study. Now, the important thing to remember about Mr. Naset's tests is that he likes lists."

"Lists?" echoed Liz.

"Right. Whenever he gives you three points to remember about, say, the reason the colonists came to America—be sure to learn them. He'll definitely ask them on a test."

"Okay," Liz said with a definite lack of enthusiasm.

"Did you copy my notes into your notebook?" Jana asked.

Liz shook her head. "I'm going to do that now."

"Oh," Jana said. She was disappointed. Why hadn't Liz copied them before she came? They could have spent this time studying together. And, come to think of it, she could have been studying on her own during the last two days if she'd had her notes to study. Liz certainly hadn't been very considerate. And now, Liz would just sit there by herself and copy the notes, which would take her at least half an hour.

Liz opened both notebooks and sat down on the floor, working on the coffee table as she began copying the notes.

"Would you like a Coke?" Jana asked.

"Sure," said Liz.

"Diet or regular?"

Liz looked up. "Regular."

"How about if I make some popcorn, too?" Jana suggested.

"Suit yourself."

Jana exhaled loudly. She didn't care if Liz knew how exasperated she was. In the kitchen she found her mother pouring herself a diet soda.

"How's it going?" she whispered.

Jana frowned. "Okay, I guess. But she sure knows how to get to me. And she didn't copy my notes, so she has to do it now."

Jana's mother nodded sympathetically and padded softly back to the bedroom. Jana filled two glasses with ice and soda and returned to the living room. She expected to see Liz copying the notes, but when she stepped through the door, Jana saw Liz gazing at something in her hand. It looked like a photograph, but at the same instant Liz glanced up. Seeing Jana, she slipped whatever it was inside her book.

Jana set the Coke in front of Liz on the coffee table without a word. Liz didn't speak either but went back to copying the notes.

It took Liz nearly an hour to copy all of them. Finally she set her pen down and, locking her fingers, stretched her arms in front of her.

"Writer's cramp?" Jana asked, trying to sound friendly.

Liz shrugged.

"Are you ready for me to quiz you?" Jana asked.

Liz made a face. "Are you kidding?" she asked sourly. "I just finished copying the notes."

"Oh, okay," Jana said. "Do you just want to study by yourself, then?"

"That's the idea," Liz said sarcastically.

"Okay," Jana said wearily. Old, ornery Liz is back, she thought. Jana picked up her own notes and curled up on the couch to study. For the next hour, Jana and Liz studied their notes silently, never speaking. Jana peeked over at Liz several times. She couldn't help wondering if Liz really had been looking at a picture, and if so, who was in it. But Liz seemed to be concentrating pretty hard on the notes in front of her. Still, the third time Jana looked at her, she noticed that Liz's eyes weren't moving.

How can you read and study if you don't move your eyes? Liz *wasn't* studying, Jana realized. She was just sitting there staring at the page, *pretending* to study!

"Would you like me to quiz you?" Jana asked. She knew she was setting a trap for Liz, but she didn't care.

"No, I gotta go," Liz said abruptly. She got up and zipped her jacket.

"Oh, well . . . " Jana fumbled. "Uh, I'll get Pink to drive you home."

"Don't bother," Liz mumbled. Without another word, she walked to the door, opened it, and disappeared down the hall.

Jana stood in the middle of the living room with her mouth open in surprise. "I can't believe it," she muttered to herself.

"Jana, did I hear someone go out?" her mother called from the bedroom.

Jana trudged back to where her mother and Pink were sitting on the bed watching TV. "I can't believe it," she repeated. "Liz came, copied my notes, drank a Coke, studied by herself, and then left! All without a thank-you, or I'll-see-you-tomorrow or good-bye." She flopped down on the end of their bed.

"That's too bad," Jana's mother said, shaking her head. "I guess Liz just isn't ready to make her own friends yet."

"Well, I've had it with her!" Jana said angrily. "I've done everything I can think of! I've shown her around school, introduced her to my friends, eaten lunch with her, given her my notes—which I could have been studying myself—and offered to help her study. And all I've gotten in return is *rudeness*!"

"I agree with you, honey," her mother said. "If you ask me, you've been awfully patient."

"You bet I've been patient!" Jana cried. "I've waited and waited for her to decide to be nice! I *know* she's had a hard life, and I *know* she doesn't have a home, and I *know* she wants to get out of the shelter! But *I* didn't put her there!" Jana sighed wearily. "I'm going to take a shower."

As she left her parents' room and entered her own, the phone rang. Pink answered it.

"Jana," Pink called. "It's for you."

"Thanks. I'll get it in the living room." When she

picked up the receiver, she made a face at it and said, "Hello."

"Hi, Jana. This is Melanie."

Jana's shoulders sagged. "Oh, hi, Mel." She wished Melanie hadn't picked this moment to call. She wasn't in the mood to talk right now.

"I just wanted to tell you what happened to me today," Melanie said anxiously, "and get your advice."

Jana sighed. "Okay," she said, "but I'm really tired, Mel, so could you make it kind of fast?"

"Well, sure," Melanie said, sounding a little hurt. "I'll make it fast, I promise." She immediately rushed into her story, speaking nonstop. "You see, it was after school, and I was walking down the sidewalk, and along came Shane on his bike, and I was thinking about the love test, and I was kind of afraid that he wouldn't speak because the test said that he'd hate me for four long, miserable years, and so I said, 'Hello!' just like that, and he turned around and waved a little, and I guess that kind of gave me confidence that maybe things weren't going to be so bad after all, and I remembered the incantation I read about in a book of folklore at the library that's supposed to cancel any kind of spell, and I said in this really loud voice—I kind of yelled it, in fact—'Spider's web and kitten's bell, I command that you remove this spell!' and, oh, man, Shane looked at me as if he thought I was totally crazy, and, Jana, no kidding, I just wanted to crawl into a hole and die!"

Melanie stopped and panted a moment. "Do you think I did the wrong thing?"

"Yes, I think you did the wrong thing!" Jana exploded. "I keep *telling* you that the love test is just a silly game, but you refuse to believe me. And *of course*, Shane is going to think you're nuts if you yell dumb things like that at him! *Anybody'd* think you were nuts! Now, if you'll excuse me, Melanie, I had kind of a bad day, and I'm going to take a shower and go to bed, okay?"

"Okay," Melanie said in a little voice. "Sorry." She hung up.

Jana sighed and trudged back to her room and flopped onto the bed. Why did I treat Melanie that way? she thought. Mel didn't deserve it.

Jana rolled over on her back and stared at the ceiling. She visualized Melanie yelling that stupid incantation at Shane and laughed out loud. Shane must have thought she'd popped a screw loose in her brain somewhere.

Poor Melanie, Jana thought. She needs a friend, not another problem.

Jana sighed. She hadn't been very nice to Melanie. She was just so frustrated with Liz! Melanie was a good friend, though, and Jana knew that she would—

Jana sat upright. What had she just done? She was upset about a problem and had treated Melanie rudely, just as Liz had treated *her* rudely during this terrible time in her life. And Liz certainly had bigger problems than Jana.

"Oh, brother," she said aloud. "I'm just as bad as Liz."

Jana went back to the living room, picked up the receiver, and dialed Melanie's number.

"Hello, Melanie?" she said. "I'm calling to apologize . . . "

Already, Jana felt better.

CHAPTER

10

"**I**'m so glad we're having this meeting," Whitney said, slipping into one of the front row seats in the auditorium. "I'm coming unglued! Leslie is just as quiet and sulky as she was the first day!"

"Yeah," said Jana, sinking into the seat next to her. "Liz won't talk much either, even the few times when she's not angry."

- Mr. Bell and Mrs. Brenner sat informally on the edge of the stage. The four remaining student partners entered the auditorium within a few minutes and seated themselves in the first two rows.

"Well," Mr. Bell began, "we thought it might be a good idea to get together today and talk about how our new program is going. Any problems? Have you learned anything helpful?"

74

Kyle Zimmerman spoke up. "I've learned that my student hates school and likes to pick fights."

"Oh, yes," Mr. Bell said. "Your partner was one of the boys who was suspended for fighting, wasn't he?"

"Yeah," Kyle said. "I called the shelter last night, and the supervisor told me that he and his mom have left town. I guess his mom was going to look for work."

"That's typical," Mrs. Brenner said. "Homeless people move around a lot looking for shelter and jobs.

"Yes, Whitney," said Mrs. Brenner.

"Leslie is really hard to deal with," Whitney said softly. "I thought she'd become a friend, but she acts as if she *hates* me. She doesn't want to talk or do anything with me. If I offer to help her with homework or with a problem she's having in class, she gets very quiet and acts angry."

"How about you, Jana?" Mr. Bell asked. "Are you having problems, too?"

Jana nodded. "My friends and I have tried to get Liz interested in extracurricular activities, but she gets really sarcastic and says those things are dumb."

"Do you think she really believes what she's saying?" Mrs. Brenner asked.

"Oh, yes," Jana said. "I think the idea of trying out for cheerleading or the school play seems stupid to her. Sometimes I've wondered if Liz is on another, well, *plane* than the rest of us."

"You mean another *planet*?" Tim said, and everybody laughed.

"No," Jana replied, "I mean that Liz and her mother are really trying hard to survive in the world. They're thinking about a place to stay, a good job, food, that sort of thing, and I suppose that, compared with those things, cheerleading and acting in a play does sound pretty silly."

"I think you're absolutely right," Mrs. Brenner said, smiling at Jana.

"So, how do we get her interested in school?" asked Jana.

"Maybe we don't," offered Pam. "Maybe all we can hope to do is try and make the school as pleasant a place as we can. Then it's up to them to do the rest."

"Right," said Jana. "And I'm not really sure that I even *want* to do much more. I mean, I try and try. I even asked her to come over to my house to study. She just couldn't be less interested in being a friend—or even *having* a friend!"

"Pam's right," Mrs. Brenner said. "We can only do so much. We can offer help, friendship, guidance—and if the students want to take advantage of those things, fine. If they don't, that's too bad. There's only so much you can do."

"Is anybody having a good experience?" Mr. Bell asked.

Tim Riggs sat forward. "Yes," he said. "My student is really a great guy."

"How long has he been homeless?" Jana asked.

"Just a few weeks," Tim said. "And his parents have already lined up jobs. They won't be at Phoenix House very long."

"Maybe he doesn't feel so bad about what he's going through, then," Jana said. "I mean, since he knows everything will be okay very soon."

"Yeah," Tim said. "You're probably right."

"I'm sure the anger and withdrawal you other people have been seeing is due to the shame and embarrassment of being homeless," said Mrs. Brenner.

"I'll bet part of it," Kyle interjected, "is the way some of the kids here at Wakeman have been treating them. I've heard some kids say pretty mean things to the students from the shelter. I walked into my science class the other day and overheard a kid call my student 'Homeless Joe.' He thought he was being really cool, I guess."

"Some kids have been saying things to me like, Why don't these people get jobs?" said Jana.

"Right," said Whitney. "Some kids have said they think these homeless people are just lazy, and they don't see why we're trying to help them."

"Well, I'm sure there *are* some lazy homeless people getting help from local agencies," said Mrs. Brenner. "There will always be people who abuse the system. But there are a great many more who desperately want work but, for one reason or another, don't have jobs or can't find them. Some have been laid off. Others have had other misfortunes. Some of them have difficulty holding jobs because of personal problems."

"Like drinking or drugs?" asked Pam.

"Yes, and other illnesses," said Mrs. Brenner. "Remember, addiction is a disease and it takes a very strong, very determined person to stay off drugs or alcohol. When there are serious financial problems or other troubles, it's hard to feel strong and determined."

"Does anyone have a suggestion about how we can do a better job helping our students?" asked Mr. Bell.

No one spoke.

"I think," Jana said slowly, "we all feel as if we are doing the best job we can."

Mr. Bell smiled. "I think you are, too. And no one can ask you to do more than that." He looked around at the students sitting in front of him. "Any more comments? Questions?"

The students shook their heads.

"So, that's it? The meeting's over?" asked Tim, looking astonished.

"I'm afraid there are no easy answers," Mrs. Brenner said.

"If there were easy answers, we'd be the first to give them to you," Mr. Bell assured them.

Jana, Whitney, and the others stood up and began walking up the auditorium aisle. Whitney walked ahead of everyone in deep thought. Then she turned around and waited for Jana.

"I thought Mr. Bell and Mrs. Brenner were going to tell us how to handle these problems. At least give us some ideas."

"Me, too." Jana sighed. "I guess principals and guidance counselors shouldn't be expected to have magic answers to every problem."

Whitney shrugged. "I guess you're right. So . . . we struggle on, right?"

Jana smiled. "Right. But I don't know what more I can do for Liz."

"Me, either," Whitney said. "I guess Pam was right. We do what we can to help them. But then *they* have to make some effort, too."

Jana swallowed a lump in her throat. "You know, I'm beginning to dread seeing Liz because I know that no matter what I do, she'll make me as miserable as she is."

Whitney nodded.

"Well," Jana said, "I'm going to try to stop worrying. If Liz's nice, we'll be friends. If not, I'll leave her alone."

Whitney waved good-bye, and Jana turned and walked down the hall toward Mr. Naset's class.

Jana had meant it when she told Whitney that she wouldn't let Liz get to her any more. But as she got near her classroom, her stomach rolled over as she thought about sitting down next to Liz.

CHAPTER

11

*T*he history test was in progress when Jana walked into the classroom. She gave her late pass to Mr. Naset, and he handed her a test.

"You have thirty minutes left," said the teacher in a low voice. "You should be able to finish before the end of the period."

Jana nodded and took the test to her seat in the back. Liz was sitting at the desk in front of her. She looked up and rolled her eyes as if to say that the test was hard.

Jana smiled and sat down, thinking that during a test, all the kids were in the same boat. It drew the students together. Even Liz.

Jana pulled a pen out of her schoolbag and scanned the paper in front of her. Sure enough, Mr.

Naset had asked several questions about the lists he'd given in class notes. Jana was glad she had warned Liz about studying lists.

Jana answered the first ten questions without much difficulty. They were fill-in-the-blank statements that could be really hard if you hadn't studied, but she had.

She had just begun a set of multiple-choice questions when Liz shifted in the seat ahead of her. Liz stretched her arms out to the sides, then leaned back in her seat. She turned her face to the side and glanced back over her shoulder. Her eyes moved over Jana's test paper.

Jana frowned and shifted her paper down a little on her desk, resting her arm over it so that Liz couldn't see the questions she was answering. After all, she thought, I worked hard studying for this test. I offered to help Liz study and loaned her my notes. But I'm not going to let her copy my test!

Liz made a little noise of frustration and anger, and turned back to her own paper.

Jana answered the multiple-choice questions, then paused and turned her attention to Liz. Liz was not working on the test anymore. She had her head down on her folded arms.

Apparently, Liz had given up. Plain and simple. Jana sighed, glad that she hadn't let Liz cheat by copying her paper. Mrs. Brenner and Mr. Bell had been right at the meeting. She could only go so far to help Liz. The rest was up to her.

Just before the bell rang, Mr. Naset collected all the tests. As the kids headed for the door, Jana grabbed her book bag and hurried out, hoping to avoid Liz. How could Liz possibly expect her to cheat? It was the last straw.

"Jana?" Liz called out.

Jana kept walking.

"Hey, Morgan, I want to talk to you."

Liz's voice had a menacing sound, which made Jana angrier than ever. She whirled around, stopping so abruptly that Liz almost plowed into her.

"Liz, I've tried to help you all I could, but—"

"But you'll only do certain things," Liz said sarcastically.

Jana could feel the anger well up inside. *Stay cool*, she reminded herself. *Don't let her get you mad*.

"Look, Morgan, I've had it with your *help*," Liz said.

"What do you mean?" Jana demanded.

The two girls were stopped in the middle of the hall while the rush of students veered around them in their hurry to get to their next classes.

"What do you *think* I mean?" Liz challenged. "You keep wanting to be Little Miss Helpful, Little Miss Fix-It, right? Well, the one time I really *need* help getting through a ridiculously hard test, you decide you're too good to help me. 'Just let her drown,' you probably thought, right?"

"What are you talking about?" Jana demanded, hearing her own voice rising and knowing she was losing her cool, but not really caring. "I've offered you help since the day you arrived in this school! If I *was* Little Miss Fix-It, as you call me, I was only trying to help you get involved in things so you could enjoy yourself a little bit. I've introduced you to my friends, offered to help you get involved in school activities, given you my notes to study, invited you over to my house to help you get ready for this test—and what do I get in return? You're sarcastic and rude to my friends, mean to me, and then you want me to *cheat* for you! Well, I'll tell you something, Liz Flagg. I don't cheat for *anybody*, you get that? I wouldn't cheat for my very best friend in the whole world, and do you know why? Because I wouldn't be doing her any favors by letting her cheat, that's why. And I'll tell you something else, Liz. I don't like it when people *use* me! And expecting me to cheat for you is *using* me!"

"Using you!" Liz cried. "I've never used anybody in my *life*! You keep shoving yourself at me constantly, trying to help this *poor, pathetic* homeless girl! Well, you know what I think every time I see you coming down the hall? I think, Oh, *great*, here comes Miss Goody Two-Shoes Morgan, ready to push her stupid little nose into my life again. I wonder how she's going to solve my problems today? Gee, maybe going out for *cheerleading* will turn my life all around, and I'll live happily ever after! Rah, RAH, *RAH*!"

"I was *hardly* pushing my nose into your business!" Jana shouted back. "I haven't asked you any personal questions about your life!"

"You treat me like a charity case!" Liz yelled. "You and all the teachers—"

"A *charity* case!"

"Look," Liz said, her voice lower but seething with anger, "my mother and I may not have a home right now, but we're hard-working and smart, and we don't need your handouts, okay? I had plenty of friends in my old school before we had to move. I don't need you or anybody else to take me by the hand and do me the *favor* of being my friend!"

"I wasn't doing you a *favor*," Jana said angrily, realizing that the hallway was clear now, and she hadn't even heard the bell. Their teachers would want an explanation about their lateness, but this conversation was more important at the moment. At least Liz was *talking* about what she was angry about! "Okay, I *did* do you one favor—loaned you my notes. Which reminds me, why didn't you study them?"

Liz snorted. "You're obviously totally stupid about shelters."

"What do you mean?"

"You're used to a quiet apartment where you have your own room and plenty of privacy," Liz said scornfully. "You couldn't hold up for one night at Phoenix House!"

"What makes you so sure?" asked Jana.

"Ha! I'd like to see you *try*!"

Jana looked Liz straight in the eye. "Okay, try me," she said, pushing her chin out.

"Yeah, right." Liz chuckled and started to move down the hall. "Tell me another funny story."

Jana grabbed her sleeve. "No, I mean it," she said stubbornly. "Let me come and spend *one night* there."

An expression of alarm passed over Liz's face, but she immediately put herself in control again.

"No way," Liz said. "You couldn't handle it."

"You know what I think?" Jana said. "I think *you* couldn't handle having me there!"

"Oh, give me a break!" Liz said, looking around as if she were searching for a way to escape.

"Then let me come," Jana insisted.

"You're crazy," Liz muttered.

"Okay! So I'm crazy!" Jana said. "Let me come— *if you can take it.*"

"Okay!" Liz said between clenched teeth. "We'll just see how you do. Come at seven tonight. And bring that all-important homework with you!"

"Oh, Jana, wait up!" Melanie called out, running down the sidewalk after school. "I've *got* to talk to you!"

"What's up, Mel?" Jana asked, turning to greet her friend.

"I saw Richie in the hall today at school!" Melanie said. "I've managed to avoid him most of the week, but he loomed up out of nowhere this afternoon while I was on my way to math class."

"Yeah? What happened?" Jana asked.

Melanie looked worried. "Well, he asked me whether I was going to Bumpers today after school!"

"Are you?"

Melanie's eyes got big. "Are you kidding! I wouldn't go *near* that place if Richie Corrierro's going to be there! I know he's hoping I'll be there so he can ask me out."

"Now, Melanie," Jana said patiently, "maybe he was just making conversation."

Melanie shook her head seriously. "Not with that expression on his face."

"What expression?" Jana asked.

"Oh, you know what I mean," Melanie said, leaning close to Jana and speaking confidentially. "He looks straight into my eyes and just hangs there looking like a lovesick cocker spaniel. You know the look. It's really pathetic. Especially on Richie Corrierro."

Jana chuckled. "I can't believe Richie could have an expression like that. He has the permanent look of someone who's about to play a practical joke. And he usually *is* about to play a joke on someone."

"Well, today he looked lovestruck," Melanie insisted. "On Shane or Garrett, that expression would have been wonderful, but on Richie, it looked awful. I thought I was going to throw up, right there in the middle of the hall."

"So what did you tell him?" Jana asked.

"I told him I had too much homework. Can you believe that? Me, not going to Bumpers because I have to study?"

"Well, come on then," Jana said. "We'll walk together."

"But you don't get it!" Melanie said, taking a step backward.

"What do you mean?" asked Jana.

"What if this happens every day?" Melanie wailed. "What if he asks me every day if I'm going to Bumpers, and every day I don't go just so I won't have to see him?"

"You wouldn't do that, would you?" Jana asked.

"Of course I would. Don't you get it? I don't want to go out with him!" Melanie whined. "But then I'll miss seeing all my friends at Bumpers."

"You don't *have* to go out with him," Jana insisted. "If he asks you out, just tell him you're busy. If it happens a couple of times, he'll get the message."

"Jana, you still don't get it, do you? Even if I turn Richie down, no one, *especially* Shane, will ask me out. That stupid love test will see to that. My cousin *proved* it. She said the name of the guy she liked, and they've been going steady ever since."

"Look," said Jana. "How can I convince you that the love test is nothing but a hoax? What would have to happen to prove to you the test has no power?"

Melanie thought a moment. "If Shane asked me

out, or Garrett, or somebody else really cute, I guess I'd be convinced."

"Terrific," said Jana. "Just plan to be at Bumpers tomorrow after school, okay? Maybe your luck will change."

Melanie looked wary for an instant. "Only if The Fabulous Five all sit together so that you guys can protect me from Richie."

Jana grinned. "Isn't that what friends are for?"

CHAPTER

12

*J*ana's mother dropped Jana off in front of Phoenix House a little after seven that evening. A frown crossed her mother's face as she looked at the old building that had once been a residence.

"I hope things go okay for you," her mother said, sounding worried. "And have a good night, honey."

"I will," Jana assured her even though her stomach was feeling nervous.

Mrs. Morgan waved as she pulled away from the curb, leaving Jana standing on the sidewalk.

Jana knew her mother wasn't too happy about her daughter's staying overnight in a shelter for the homeless. At first her mother had said, *"You're doing what?"*

"I'm going to stay at Phoenix House with Liz," Jana repeated.

"I'm not sure it's a good idea," her mother had said. "What about your homework? How will you get your studying done?" It sounded as if she were searching for reasons why Jana shouldn't go.

"The same way Liz does hers," answered Jana. She hoped her mother wouldn't ask how *that* was.

"What kind of sleeping arrangements do they have there? Will you have any privacy?" her mother had asked.

"Mom," Jana had responded, "the whole reason I'm going to stay overnight with Liz is to see how she has to live. She says I have no idea what it's like to live in a shelter, and she's right. I think this will be *good* for me. You know . . . a learning experience."

A smile had crept across Jana's mother's face. "It seems as if I've heard that argument before. I've used it on you a few times, haven't I?"

Jana had giggled. "Yes, you have. It's a pretty good one too, isn't it?"

Her mother had shaken her head. "Okay. But let me talk to whoever is in charge over there first. Then we'll make a decision."

Mrs. Pinkerton had called the supervisor of Phoenix House, whose name turned out to be Nathan, asking him every conceivable question. When she hung up she had a satisfied look on her face.

Jana walked slowly up the sidewalk leading to the front steps of the gray two-story building. Across the front of the house was a big screened-in porch. The building was old but the wood siding looked as if it had been recently painted. All in all, Phoenix House looked better than the neighboring houses, some of which were pretty run-down and had overgrown yards.

Jana walked up the front steps and hesitated at the screened door. Should she knock, or go on in and knock at the inner door? She decided that no one would hear if she knocked where she was, so she opened the door and went in.

Standing next to the heavy glass paned door that led into the house, Jana could hear voices. Curtains kept her from seeing inside. She felt suddenly shy. Phoenix House was really home for the people who lived there. Would they think of her as an intruder? Would they resent her being there? Suddenly she felt like turning around and leaving. Maybe there was a phone booth at the corner, and she could call her mother to come and get her.

No. If she did that, she wouldn't be able to face Liz in the morning. She could just see the look on Liz's face if Jana didn't show up after the big argument they had had.

Jana resolutely pushed the doorbell and waited for someone to answer. She heard the sound of running and the door was jerked open by a little boy who looked about six years old.

"Hi," Jana said. "Is Liz Flagg here?"

"Yeah," the boy said. He obviously had a bad

cold. His nose was running and he was sniffling. Jana was tempted to get a tissue out of her purse and wipe the mess on his face for him, but she didn't.

The boy just stood staring at her.

"Do you think I could come in?" Jana asked.

"Guess so," the boy said, stepping back.

"Josh!" came a voice from inside the house. "You remember the rules."

A pleasant-looking man with blue eyes and brown hair that was thin on the top but grew down over his ears appeared at the door.

"Josh, you know no one answers the door but me," said the man firmly.

"Hi," the man said to Jana. "I keep telling Josh about the answering-the-door rule, but he never seems to remember." He stuck out his hand. "I'm Nathan, the director of Phoenix House. Can I help you?"

"Hello. I'm Jana Morgan," she said.

"Oh, yes. Your mother called. You're Liz's friend. Come on in."

Jana followed him into the big entryway. Directly in front of her was a wide staircase that went upstairs. To one side of it was a hallway leading back into the house, and there were doors both to the left and right that led into other rooms.

"I'm really sorry," said Nathan. "I checked after I talked to your mother, and Liz and her family aren't here at the moment. I believe they went to the church down the block for supper. We provide breakfast every day and lunch on weekends, but the residents have to get their own suppers. Most of them go to the church. You can wait for Liz in the TV room, if you'd like. It's down the hallway on the right."

Jana thanked him and found the TV room. Inside, two women sat together on a worn couch and stared at the television while Josh, and two other children who looked like preschoolers, played noisily on the floor at their feet. Everyone looked up when Jana walked in.

"Hi," Jana said shyly.

"Hi," the women responded, and immediately went back to watching TV.

The show was a rerun of *The Andy Griffith Show*, and, not knowing what else to do, Jana took a seat in an oversized chair with springs that had seen much better days.

On the screen, deputy Barney was confronting bank robbers and trembling all over with excitement as he searched frantically for the one bullet the sheriff had given him so he could load his gun. Jana giggled as he looked in one pocket after the other for the bullet, but the faces of the women on the couch never changed. No laughs . . . not even a smile. They just stared at the set, their eyes blank.

The children started climbing onto another overstuffed chair and jumping off and rolling on the floor, all the while squealing at the tops of their lungs. Their yelling grew louder as they played until

Jana had to cover her ears. She looked at the women, expecting them to say something to the kids, but all that happened was one of them got up, turned up the sound on the television, and sat down again.

Jana wished Liz would come back as the kids started pushing and shoving one another all over the room. Had Liz remembered that Jana was coming over? Maybe she did and this was her way of getting even with Jana for what she had said in the hallway at school.

Halfway into the next sitcom, when Jana was sure her ears were going to burst, she heard someone call her name. Looking around, she saw Liz looking at her from the doorway. Liz jerked her head in a motion for Jana to follow, and then disappeared.

Jana grabbed her bag and purse, hopped over the three kids and went through the door after her.

"Wait up," Jana called as Liz walked hurriedly down the hall. Liz's stiff back gave no indication that she had heard Jana.

Jana caught up with her midway up the squeaking staircase to the second floor.

"So you didn't cop out after all," Liz said sarcastically without looking at Jana.

"I told you I would come," Jana answered, anger rising inside her. "If you can stay here, I can too."

"Humph!" said Liz as she continued up the stairs and in through a door.

Jana followed and found herself inside a large room with army cots along one wall. Two women were sitting on cots at one end of the room and a woman with a small girl was unrolling the mattress on another in the opposite corner. The empty beds had mattresses rolled up like jelly rolls on them. On the other side of the room, a fireplace with an elegant mantel was sealed off with plywood, and the windows at the ends of the room were covered by dilapidated-looking blinds that had wide slats. Liz headed toward the woman and child.

"You met my mom," Liz said gruffly when they reached the lady. Jana recognized her from that day in school when she was introduced to Liz. Mrs. Flagg was making a bed and had two large shopping bags stuffed with things at her feet. Jana realized that they probably contained everything that the Flagg family owned.

"Hello, Mrs. Flagg," Jana said politely.

Liz's mother gave her a half smile and returned to making the bed.

"This is my sister, Martha," Liz said, putting her hand on the little girl's head.

Martha gave Jana a much bigger smile and seemed happy to see her.

"The women and children sleep up here," said Liz. "The men sleep downstairs. They've also got a couple of rooms downstairs for families that have both parents so they can stay together. You can have that bed," she said, indicating one that was fourth from the end. "Everyone tries to get a corner so they can have more privacy."

"Thanks," said Jana. Liz didn't bother to reply.

There was a blanket, a pillow, two sheets, and a pillowcase stacked on the cot. Jana rolled the mattress out over the wire springs and made the bed. The name "Phoenix House" was written on the tattered edges of the sheets and pillowcase with a black marker. It was probably to help keep people from taking them.

When she was finished, Jana took off her coat and sat on her cot waiting for Liz to finish making hers.

As she was waiting, other women came into the room carrying shopping bags and paper sacks, some with children, some without. Jana was shocked to see one lady who appeared to be about the same age as her own Grandma Morgan. She had never thought of her grandmother in any way except bustling around in her kitchen making good smells in the house that she and Grandpa Morgan had lived in most of their lives. It was hard for Jana to draw her eyes away from the woman. She might be someone's grandma, too.

"Well, are you ready to do homework?" Liz's voice startled Jana. She turned, and Liz was standing over her, the same angry look on her face.

"Sure," said Jana, digging her books out of her bag. "I'll just stuff these things under my bed," she said, zipping the bag shut.

"You'd better not," Liz warned. "Put it under Mom's bed. She'll be here to watch it. And you better not leave your coat lying there, either. If you do, it won't be here when you get back."

The thought that someone might steal her things if she wasn't careful made Jana's skin crawl. She had never had to worry about that before. She did as Liz told her and put her bag under Mrs. Flagg's bed and put her coat back on. *Now* Jana understood why Liz wouldn't take her coat off at school.

"It's too dark to study up here," Liz said, nodding toward the single light bulb in the middle of the ceiling. She was right, it couldn't have been more than sixty-watts.

Outside the room, Liz pointed to a half-opened door at the end of the hall. "That's the only bathroom on this floor," she said. "You can take a bath tonight or in the morning, suit yourself. But you may have to wait your turn. There's no shower . . . just a tub . . . and you'll have to scrub it out for the next person when you finish."

Liz led Jana back down the stairs and along the narrow hall beside the stairway. "This is the play-room," she said as they turned into a small room. "We can study in here while the kids are in the TV room. Sometimes, when there's a test coming up in school, I have to study in the laundry room. That's only when there aren't too many people doing laun-dry, of course." She said it in a matter-of-fact way and not with any anger.

There was a large couch in the room. Its back was split and the arms frayed. Against one wall was a rickety bookcase with children's books. A child-sized table and chairs sat next to it, and a closet stood open revealing a jumble of toys. Jana and Liz took seats on the opposite ends of the couch.

As they were settling in to do their homework, Jana heard the doorbell ring and Nathan shout, "Josh, don't you *dare* open that door!"

"Why can't Josh open the door?" Jana asked.

Liz stared at her. "It's the rule," she said. "I guess some mothers and kids have stayed here in the past to get away from violent husbands. Nathan's the one who answers the door just in case it's one of those men."

Jana shrunk down a little on the couch. She hadn't thought that there might be violence associated with staying at a shelter. Shelters were supposed to be places where people could come and find a place to stay where it was safe. She watched Liz as she concentrated on her homework.

Just then there was the thunder of footsteps running in the hall, and Josh and the two little girls he had been playing with appeared in the doorway along with two more children.

"Lizzie, where've you been!" yelled Josh as they rushed into the room squealing.

"Play with us, Lizzie!" the children shouted, jumping up and down.

"Well, so much for studying," Liz said ruefully. "Look, kids, I've got company and I have to study. Can't you play by yourselves?"

"Awww," said one of the little girls.

"I know," said another. "Let's play eviction."

"I'm gonna be the daddy!" yelled the littlest girl.

"*I'm* gonna be the daddy!" shouted Josh. "You be the sheriff."

"Okay, Angela, you be the sheriff," said one girl who appeared to be the oldest, "and I'll be the mommy. Anna, you be the kid."

"Okay," said Josh, sitting down at the little table. "This'll be the house, and we're at home eating supper."

They all took what looked like preassigned places, and Angela stomped into what was supposed to be the "house."

Jana watched in amazement at what must have been a game the children played lots of times.

"YOU HAVE TO LEAVE!" little Angela roared as loudly as she could. "I'm evicting you!"

"No! No!" cried the "mommy." She pretended to cry, "*Wahh! Wahh! I don't want to lose my home!*"

"*I'm not leaving my house!*" Josh-Daddy shouted.

"You leave peacefully, or I'll throw you out!" Angela yelled. The words seemed even more preposterous coming from such a cute little girl.

Jana stared speechless as she watched the children play their *eviction* game. The very idea that three-to-six-year-olds would even know what the word meant was incredible. But they all obviously understood very well what getting evicted was all about, as they went about playing their roles. They've actually seen people get thrown out of their homes, Jana thought in amazement.

Red-faced and angry, Liz looked at Jana and stood up abruptly. "Come on, you guys. That's not a good game to be playing. Let's do something else."

"What? What?" the kids shouted as they jumped up and down, ready for a new game.

"How about a story?" Liz suggested.

"Yea! I love Lizzie's stories!" Angela cried.

"Tell the one about the three bears," cried Josh. "That's a good one."

"Yeah! The three bears!" shouted Anna.

"Okay, you guys," said Liz, sliding to the floor. "Gather around me."

The children quickly settled cross-legged in a circle around Liz and looked up at her with wide eyes as she started the story.

"Once upon a time there were three bears. The papa bear, the mama bear, and the little baby bear . . ."

Jana took a deep breath and leaned back to watch Liz tell her story. Liz's face lit up, her body became animated, and her eyes sparkled as she led the children into the fairy tale. The kids sat silent, hanging on every word that she said.

Jana was astonished at how great Liz was with the kids. She had said she loved them, and it was obvious that she did, and they loved her, too. Maybe Liz could become a teacher someday and use her talent with young children.

Jana thought about the last couple of weeks with Liz at school: Liz's not wanting to be friends with anyone, not getting her homework done, not wanting to get involved at Wakeman. Now, sitting here watching Liz entertain kids in the shelter so they wouldn't play the eviction game, everything seemed to really make sense for the first time.

Liz was a very proud and capable girl. She and her family had simply had bad luck. Now Liz had to live in a place where she had to watch her things all the time to keep them from being stolen, she didn't have a place to study, she had to live in a big room with a lot of other people, and there was even the danger that some violent husband might come barging into the shelter looking for his family.

Jana shivered. She really had to admire Liz for being able to handle so many tough things. When you looked at it that way, Jana wondered if she could do as well if she, her mother, and Pink were in the same situation. She guessed probably not.

As Liz finished telling her story, Jana slid down onto the floor next to her. "Have you guys heard the one about Snow White and the seven dwarfs?" Jana asked.

"Yeah! But tell it anyway," said Anna.

As Jana started her story, the kids turned their attention to her. Out of the corner of her eye, Jana noticed Liz looking at her curiously.

CHAPTER

13

*L*ater, after the kids had all been put to bed and Jana and Liz had finished studying, the two girls made their way back upstairs.

"You were really super with those kids, Liz," Jana said.

"You weren't too bad with them yourself," Liz replied. "It's after ten o'clock, which is when they make us turn out the lights in the sleeping rooms. You'll have to get dressed in the dark."

"I hope I don't get my pajama tops and bottoms mixed up," Jana said, giggling.

Liz glanced at her and actually had a small smile on her face. "It's a good thing we made our beds before we came down or we might have had to sleep on a bare mattress."

"What time can you get back into the shelter during the day?" Jana asked as they stopped outside the dormitory door.

"Four-thirty in the afternoon," said Liz.

"But school's out between three-fifteen and three-thirty," Jana protested. "What do you do between then and four-thirty?"

Liz shrugged. "Sometimes I meet my mother at the library or I go to the YWCA and help take care of the little kids in the day-care center."

"Really?" said Jana. "I didn't know that. Is your mother having any luck finding a job?"

Liz's face brightened. "She had an interview today that she thought went real well, and she heard that the factory where she used to work may be calling people back."

"I'll be keeping my fingers crossed for her," Jana said, showing both her hands with fingers crossed. "I'd do my toes, too, if I could."

Liz's face softened. "Thanks."

Later, Jana lay on her cot trying to sleep. Along the row of beds, several people were snoring in different keys, and it was distracting. At the other end of the room someone was coughing. She was used to her own room, which was totally silent when everyone went to bed. Every time she rolled over trying to find a more comfortable way of lying on the bumpy mattress the springs would squeak so loudly she was afraid it would waken Liz, who was in the bed next to her.

A streak of moonlight came through the space between the edge of the blind and the window frame
and fell across Liz's face. She was sleeping, but every
once in a while Jana saw her frown and move. What
kind of dreams must she be having? Jana wondered.
Her whole world is turned upside down. As she lay
looking at Liz, a tear rolled out of Jana's eye and
down her cheek.

Children's voices in the hall woke Jana the next
morning. She was still groggy from not being able to
sleep because of the noise in the night, and she
pulled the cover up over her head.

"Better get up," she heard Liz say.

Jana peeked out. Liz was already dressed and
making her bed. Mrs. Flagg was not in the room.

"Sleep well?" Liz asked, smiling at Jana. Jana
wasn't sure whether she was being sarcastic or not.
She decided she wasn't.

"Well, not exactly," Jana answered, struggling to
sit up and scratching her itchy head. "I've got to
hand it to you, Liz. Sleeping in a place like this is
heroic."

"It's pretty noisy, isn't it?"

"To say the least." Jana looked Liz in the eyes. "I
want you to know I'm sorry about the way things
went studying for the history test. I didn't understand how practically impossible it is for you to
study in this place."

Liz nodded. "That's okay. This place isn't easy to imagine." She drew in a deep breath. "I guess I was pretty hard on you, too. But you had *better* get in gear if you're going to get cleaned up at all. There's probably a line a mile long at the john right now."

"Oh, my gosh!" said Jana, jumping up. "I forgot."

Quickly she dug through her bag and pulled out her toothbrush, toothpaste, hairbrush, and hair dryer.

"What's that?" Liz asked, smiling and pointing to the hair dryer.

"My hair dryer," responded Jana.

"I know. I'm just teasing, but you won't be able to use it in the bathroom. They don't allow electric appliances in there."

"They don't?" asked Jana. "Well, how am I going to wash my hair? It's all oily and I can't go to school with it looking this way."

"You won't have time to wash it anyway. There's a ten-minute limit on the bathroom, and that's for *everything*, including cleaning the tub for the next person. I usually wash mine when I get here after school. There's no one waiting in line then, and nobody cares if you take more time."

Jana started to protest that if she had to wash her hair the night before, it would be greasy again by the next morning, and she would look like a mess at school. But then she remembered how many times she had silently criticized Liz for her greasy hair. Criticized her before she understood. Jana kept quiet and wondered quickly if she could wrap something around her hair and wear it to school. She hated to let people see her this way. What if *Randy* saw her with her hair dirty or stringy?

"Do you have soap or a towel?" Liz asked.

"No! Should I?"

"This isn't the Marriott," Liz answered, chuckling. "They don't supply all those good things."

Jana frantically looked in her bag for something to dry with as Mrs. Flagg came back into the room.

"Mom, Jana doesn't have soap or a towel," said Liz. "Do we have an extra?"

"Sure we do," said her mother. She dug a towel and washcloth out of the shopping bag and handed them to Jana. They had been worn so thin by use, Jana wondered if the towel would sop up any water at all.

"Here, you can use my soap," said Liz. "You'll have to hurry, but if the line's not too long you should be okay. I'm going downstairs to get something to eat. When you're finished, come to the kitchen."

Armed with Liz's wet soap, the thin towel, her toothbrush and toothpaste, Jana went out into the hall. Her heart sank when she saw the line in front of the bathroom door. Three women stood or leaned against the wall in their robes waiting patiently. Jana fell in at the rear of the line.

The line moved slowly, and by the time Jana was next to use the bathroom she was hopping up and down and hoping Liz wouldn't leave for school before she was ready.

When she was finally in the bathroom, Jana opted to wash herself off with the washcloth rather than trying to take a tub bath. When she had finished, she looked at her hair. It was a stringy mess from the oil that had come out in it. Ugh! Should she run water over it and try to blow it dry in the dormitory? Her shoulders dropped in dismay. There wasn't enough time to dry it if she did. Maybe she should just go home and play sick? What would Liz think if she did? Jana knew what she would think. She would think that Jana couldn't take it. She gritted her teeth and brushed her hair up as well as she could. It didn't improve much.

Jana sighed and opened the bathroom door. A family of three was waiting their turn. She smiled and hurried back into the dormitory to put stuff away and join Liz downstairs in the kitchen.

"Did you have everything you needed?" asked Mrs. Flagg.

"Pretty much," Jana answered. What else was she going to say?

"Oh, Jana," said Mrs. Flagg. "Would you take this book to Lizzie? She forgot it."

"Sure," said Jana, hoisting the strap of her bag over her shoulder and taking it.

As she took the stair steps two at a time something fell out of the book Liz's mother had given her. Jana rolled her eyes in exasperation and reached down to pick it up. She was late enough as it was. Her hand stopped in midair. It was a photograph. Slowly Jana picked it up. Three faces smiled up at her from the picture, and one of them was Liz Flagg. Liz was in the middle, and on either side of her, arms wrapped around one another, was another girl. Liz and her friends, Jana thought, looking as close and happy as The Fabulous Five. Were they The Terrific Three? And this must be the picture Liz was looking at the night she came to Jana's apartment to study. Looking and remembering.

Jana blinked and glanced at the photo again. Why did it seem so strange to see Liz looking like a normal kid? Was it because Jana had never been able to see Liz that way, in spite of how hard she tried? Had she always thought of her as "homeless" first and as a "real person" second? Worst of all, had Liz been able to tell?

Jana slipped the picture back into Liz's book and hurried to the kitchen.

"Have some cereal. Then we've got to go," Liz said when Jana sat down beside her. Liz shoved a spoon and a single-serving box of Cheerios at Jana. "Eat it out of the box. We're out of clean dishes. Here's some milk."

Jana almost choked on her cereal. Her mind was still on the picture of Liz and her friends. She remembered at the start of the project thinking that if things had been different, she and her mother might have had to live like the Flaggs. But never in her wildest imagination had she known what it would really be like.

Within seven minutes, the girls were out the door and on their way to school. Jana glanced at Liz walking along beside her and felt a rush of admiration for her. She was in a terrible situation, but she was dealing with it extremely well, when you considered everything. Liz was a real survivor. Jana knew she was going to make it.

CHAPTER

14

"Okay, so here I am," Melanie said, plopping down in the booth at Bumpers. "Let the good times roll."

"That's the attitude, Mel," Jana said. She yawned. She'd been yawning all day and could barely keep her eyes open during classes.

Melanie rolled her eyes toward the ceiling. "I was kidding, Jana," she said. "I mean, I'll have good times with The Fabulous Five, as always, but boys . . ." Her voice trailed off sadly.

The Fabulous Five had met after school to spend some time together. They had all been so busy lately, they hadn't had a chance to see one another as much as they liked. Jana thought it was good to be together as a fivesome again. Then she was going straight home to take a long bubble bath and wash her hair.

"Don't bet on having no boys in your life," Christie told Melanie. "I heard Shane Arrington telling someone in the hall that he was coming here today."

"That doesn't mean he'll even look at me," Melanie said glumly.

"We'll see," said Katie. Then she turned to Jana. "So your overnight at the shelter went okay?"

"What was it like?" asked Beth. "Was it fun?"

"I wouldn't call it 'fun,'" said Jana. "It was certainly an eye-opener. I can see now how Liz can't get her homework done. It's very noisy, and there really isn't any place to study."

"What were the people like?" asked Christie.

"The adults were tired, mostly," Jana said. "The kids entertained themselves and got pretty loud." She paused. There was a lot more to it than that, but she wasn't really ready to talk about it yet, even to her friends. She would, though, very soon, and she knew they'd understand. "I'm glad I went," she added. "I think Liz was glad, too."

Suddenly Melanie grabbed Jana's hand. "Don't look now, but guess who just walked in the door."

"Uhm, don't tell me," Beth murmured, her hand to her forehead, pretending to think very hard. "Uhm, the name is on the tip of my tongue—don't tell me—"

Melanie's breathless whisper interrupted her. "It's *Shane Arrington*."

"Oh, you told me," Beth said, with exaggerated disappointment. Then she grinned and winked at Jana.

"He's with Randy," Melanie said. "Jana, maybe you can call Randy over, and Shane will come with him."

"Sure," said Jana. It was good to see Randy. She waved to him. "Hi, guys," she called.

Randy grinned and poked Shane in the ribs. Then the two boys sauntered toward The Fabulous Five's table. Jana felt Melanie stiffen next to her.

"Relax," Jana whispered. "Just relax and be yourself."

"Hi," said Randy. "How's it going?"

Jana gave him her best smile. "Great," she said, and nudged Melanie under the table.

"Uh, Shane," Melanie started out nervously. "How's Igor these days? I haven't heard much about him lately."

Melanie had asked about Shane's favorite subject, his pet iguana, and his face lit up. "Oh, he's awesome as usual," Shane said proudly. "He's been showing up when I experiment in the kitchen." Shane grinned. "Actually he says he's always had a secret desire to be a chef and go to the Cordon Bleu cooking school in France."

Melanie laughed. "Igor is pretty talented."

"You've got that right," Shane said. He dug into his jeans pocket. "I think I'll play a song on the jukebox. Want to help me choose one, Melanie?"

Melanie's eyes grew wide. "Oh, yes, I'd *love* to!" she said, beaming.

She got up and started across the crowded room with Shane, then glanced back over her shoulder and mouthed the word *wow!* to her friends. They all laughed.

Beth pulled Jana toward her and whispered in her ear, "You didn't say anything to Randy about Mel's love test, did you?"

Jana frowned. "Of course not," she whispered back, being sure that Randy couldn't hear.

"And you didn't just *suggest* that he talk to Shane about Melanie, did you?"

"You know me better than that," Jana said indignantly. "Whatever's happening right now is strictly Shane's idea."

Beth nodded her approval and then pointed toward the door. Liz was walking into Bumpers and heading straight for the table where the girls and Randy were sitting.

"Hi, Jana," Liz said. "I thought I might find you here."

"Liz! I'm glad you came," Jana said, smiling. "Sit down with us."

"I can't," Liz said. "Mom and I are getting ready to leave."

"Leave?" asked Jana.

Liz grinned. "We're leaving town, going back home. Mom got that job she interviewed for, and they want her to start work right away."

"Liz, that's wonderful!" Jana said, clapping her hands.

"Congratulations!" said Christie.

"Terrific," added Katie.

"Thanks, guys. Uh, Jana, could I see you alone for a sec?" Liz asked.

Jana slid out of her chair. "Sure."

Liz led Jana to a spot away from the crowd. "I just wanted to say thank you," Liz said, turning to her.

"For what?" asked Jana.

"For—well, for being a friend when I was hard to like," Liz said with a little smile.

"Hey," Jana said, "we had a rocky start, that's all."

"Well, you're a special person, Jana," Liz said. "That's why I'd like for you to have these." She pulled a tissue out of her pocket and unfolded it.

Jana gasped. "Your earrings!" she said. "Your grandmother's beautiful earrings! You can't give those to me!"

"I want you to have them. Honest," Liz said softly.

Jana started to protest again, but the look on Liz's face stopped her. She really does want me to have them, Jana thought. It's important for her to be able to give something to me.

"Thank you, Liz," Jana said, her eyes moistening as she slipped an earring into each ear. "I'll treasure them. I really will."

"Hey," Liz said with a grin, "call me Lizzie, okay?"

Jana grinned back. "Sure, Lizzie."

Lizzie leaned over and gave Jana a tight hug. "I'll write when we get settled," she said.

"And I'll write back," Jana promised, returning the hug.

"Take care," Lizzie said. "I hate good-byes, so I'll just say, 'See you later.'"

"See you," Jana said.

Lizzie held up her hand in a little wave to the rest of The Fabulous Five and disappeared out the door. Jana watched her go and felt both happy and sad. It was hard to have a friend leave, but she knew that Lizzie and her mother had a good chance of making a success of their lives. They were going home now, and Lizzie would be back with her old friends. Jana sighed and walked back to the booth.

"Sad to see her go?" Beth asked.

Jana nodded. "But I'm really glad her mother got a job. Now they can start living normal lives again."

"Uh-oh," Christie said, watching the door. "Shane just left. I hope Melanie isn't upset."

"From the look on her face," Beth said, "I'd say that her mood has improved quite a bit."

Melanie skipped up to their table, beaming. "You'll never guess what!" she said. "Shane asked me out! Can you believe it?"

"Sure," Jana said with a grin. "You're a nice girl, and Shane likes you."

"Wow!" she said, clasping her hands under her chin. "I never would have thought it was possible."

"So, now do you believe that the love test was just a silly game?" asked Jana.

"Well, I suppose so," Melanie said slowly. "On the other hand, maybe the song Shane and I chose cancelled out the love test spell."

"What song?" asked Katie.

"'Do You Believe in Magic?'" said Melanie in a dreamy voice. Then she giggled and added, "I always thought that song had some mystical qualities—"

The girls all groaned at once and then laughed. It had been a tough couple of weeks, but it was obvious that things were finally back to crazy-normal. And that's the way Jana liked life with The Fabulous Five. Crazy-normal!

CHAPTER

15

The Fabulous Five sat by the window at Bumpers finishing their sodas. Outside the street was filled with icy slush from snow that had fallen the night before and refused to melt completely as the temperature stayed around thirty-four degrees. The sky was still a dirty gray, and it matched the girls' moods.

"Jeez!" complained Beth. "There's nothing to do around this place."

"Tell me about it," said Christie. "There's no good movies on anywhere, and I looked at the TV schedule and there's nothing except reruns coming up."

"What makes it worse," joined in Katie, "is that the winter break between semesters is coming up, and it's not going to get any better."

"Over a whole week with nothing to do," sighed Melanie. "I may go stark raving mad. What are you going to do, Jana?"

"Randy and I'll probably watch a lot of reruns and eat popcorn. I'll bet I gain ten pounds before school starts again."

"What we need is something to stir up a little excitement around here," said Beth.

"Yeah," agreed Melanie, "I need some pizzazz in my life."

"You'd probably like a handsome guy to come driving up in his own three hundred ZX and sweep you off your feet," said Christie, laughing.

"Yeah," agreed Katie, "and carry you away to La La Land, where you'll live happily ever after."

"Not me," Melanie protested. "I've finally got a date with Shane, and I'm not going to take any chances of blowing it with him. But that doesn't keep me from wanting to have fun."

"Some fun doesn't sound too bad to me," said Beth. "I'm ready for it, too."

"You guys," responded Jana. "Can't you be happy with what you've got? We all have great boyfriends and as much to do as most people have. What more could we *really* want?"

"Well, a little sunshine wouldn't hurt," said Christie, looking out at the miserable weather.

"And a little variety and excitement in the things we have to do," added Katie.

*   *   *

Unbeknownst to The Fabulous Five, that's *exactly* what's going to happen during their winter break. Melanie's father wins an all-expenses-paid vacation to the island of Barbados in the Caribbean, and the whole group gets to go along. On Barbados they find lots of sunshine, palm trees, and sandy beaches, all kinds of exciting things to do, and more romance than *any* of them ever dreamed of. Don't miss The Fabulous Five Super Edition #2: *Caribbean Adventure*.

ABOUT THE AUTHOR

Betsy Haynes, the daughter of a former news-woman, began scribbling poetry and short stories as soon as she learned to write. A serious writing career, however, had to wait until after her marriage and the arrival of her two children. But that early practice must have paid off, for within three months Mrs. Haynes had sold her first story. In addition to a number of magazine short stories and the Taffy Sinclair series, Mrs. Haynes is also the author of *The Great Mom Swap* and its sequel, *The Great Boyfriend Trap.* She lives in Marco Island, Florida, with her husband, who is also an author.